SINNER

JAYNE RYLON   OPAL CAREW   AVERY ASTER

HAPPY ENDINGS PUBLISHING

Cover Art by Arijana Karčić

Editing by Mackenzie Walton

eBook & Print Formatting by Jayne Rylon

Version 2

Ebook ISBN: 978-1-941785-84-3

Print ISBN: 978-1-941785-85-0

One luxury building holds six penthouse apartments owned by kinky Manhattanites. Their sizzling stories will be told throughout the Penthouse Pleasures series from New York Times bestselling authors Opal Carew, Jayne Rylon, and Avery Aster.

Abandoning his faith gave Gabriel time to care for one of his parishioners-turned-mentor at the end of the man's long life. Following his death, Gabriel inherited priceless relics along with a luxurious Manhattan penthouse to store them in. Adrift in a city full of temptations, he has a fortune large enough to indulge any of his wicked whims.

He and his dog Goliath are settling in when the building's manager, Everly Wright, makes Gabriel feel a little too at home in his new surroundings. As he struggles to find inner peace, he begins to realize that caring for others is still part of his calling, just in an entirely new—and very erotic—way.

Lost, Gabriel seeks to regain balance in his life and decide for himself what's good for his soul...even if it makes him a sinner of the worst sort.

ADDITIONAL INFORMATION

Sign up for the Naughty News for contests, release updates, news, appearance information, sneak peek excerpts, reading-themed apparel deals, and more. www.jaynerylon.com/newsletter

Shop for autographed books, reading-themed apparel, goodies, and more www.jaynerylon.com/shop

A complete list of Jayne's books can be found at www.jaynerylon.com/books

1

———

Gabriel Hendricks kicked back in the shallows of a luxurious rooftop pool. Actual palm trees ringed by gobs of plants with broad leaves and brightly colored flowers surrounded him. A gradual sandy slope cradled his body. Cerulean water lapped over his abdomen, making it easy to image he was on a secluded tropical island instead of the top of one of Manhattan's swankiest apartment buildings, which also happened to be his private backyard.

He splayed his legs beneath gentle, if artificial, waves and soaked up the sunshine beaming directly onto him. The fact that he didn't burst into flames was somewhat reassuring. Maybe he wasn't actually the monster he considered himself lately.

Then again, he was only able to enjoy his lazy afternoon because he'd ditched his usual volunteer work. What terrible excuse for a human being would forsake helping the less fortunate so he could instead lounge around outside a world-class penthouse he'd done nothing to earn?

Gabriel, that's who.

He forced himself to relax or he'd stroke out before he could do anything to better himself. That's why he'd taken a day off, wasn't it? To get his thoughts in order and figure out what to do with the enormous opportunity he'd been given when he inherited this place and the fortune that went along with it. Maybe then he could accomplish enough good to erase the horrific mistakes of his past.

It hardly seemed real.

How had he both gained and lost so much in the past year?

His life was utterly unrecognizable from what it had been like before. It was as if a bomb had gone off, imploding every bit of his existence. When he tried to reassemble the smoking pieces, they refused to settle into place and he wasn't quite sure how—or even if—they could fit together into a cohesive whole again. He had plenty of cracks and felt barely glued together, that was for damn sure.

Theoretically, he was free. Wealthy. A man without the restrictive shackles of organized religion to keep him from indulging in whatever vices struck his fancy. Although, to be honest, none really had. Obliterating his consciousness with drugs, greedily hoarding his wealth, regularly indulging in sloth—you know, on days other than this one —those things weren't really his style.

There was only one thing with the power to tempt him at the moment.

A woman, of course.

Everly Wright was the building manager of the ridiculously upscale skyscraper he now called home. Generous and caring, she went above and beyond the customer service responsibilities of her position to make sure he and the rest of the tenants wanted for nothing. Every single afternoon since his dog Goliath had been shot by an intruder in the apartment next door, she'd come to check on him and take him for a walk while Gabriel was out volunteering.

A bunch of times she'd stayed late into the evening. Her company had become a welcome reprieve from the quiet hours of night when his confused mind tortured him from sleepless dusk to dawn. She had made excuses to hang out with both Gabriel and Goliath until she'd become the only person he considered a true friend. Though she never said as much out loud, Gabriel felt like she could sense the darkness cloaking him and was doing her best to chase it away.

It worked. When she was around he forgot about his troubles. How could he not? She was kind, bubbly, easy to talk to, optimistic, compassionate, selfless, and cute. Okay, no. She was downright sexy. Alluring. A temptress without trying to be.

As he thought of the soft, curly hair that framed her face, highlighting her sparkling green eyes and her sometimes wicked grin, his hands moved to his chest then down his abdomen toward the waistband of his ridiculously tight bathing suit.

Since he had burned his priest robes in the penthouse's gilded fireplace last year, he'd gone from ghostly pale to a golden tan almost all over. Still, he hadn't yet mustered the courage to sunbathe nude in the heart of the city, despite the fact that no one was high enough to spy on him here at the top of the world.

The tightening in his groin pushed him past his discomfort.

Gabriel shoved his thumbs beneath his waistband,

then peeled the constricting spandex off his hips and down his legs. He kicked it somewhere into the deeper water past his toes. Goliath lifted his head at the splash before going back to sleep in the shade beneath a table nearby.

Closing his eyes, Gabriel blocked out reality and focused on the vision he had of Everly. She was laughing, as she did so often. Her joy soothed his fractured spirit. It reminded him that there was more than evil at the core of some people, despite the horrors he'd witnessed.

She drew him from gloom into an emotional glow more powerful than the rays he was desperately trying to soak up in an attempt to sear away the inky black stains on his soul.

Though effective, spending time with Everly wasn't the best method for cleansing his psyche because his thoughts kept drifting to decidedly unwholesome places. Sure, he'd been curious about physical relations since puberty. He'd forcefully ignored those stray impure thoughts since he'd already been in seminary school at that time. The vow of celibacy he knew would come with his Holy Orders had made it easy to shove any corresponding urges into a neat box labeled Not-For-Me. Now, he didn't have those limitations to curb his appetites.

What would it feel like if Everly were here, brightening his morning even further by kneeling over him, her thighs spread on either side of his as she explored his body?

He rubbed the tight muscles in his legs and abdomen, feeling them flex and release beneath his fingertips. He might not have any practical experience, but his instincts were alive and well. His ass clenched, rocking his pelvis upward, thrusting his now fully erect cock at his vision of the perfect playmate.

In his imagination, Everly purred and reached for it.

Gabriel wrapped his fingers around his shaft, groaning and shifting his head from side to side on the manmade beach beneath him as he imagined the first contact of her flesh with his. She wouldn't hesitate. Everly would delight in the jump of his cock in her fist.

After stroking him several times, she might even lean down and lick the pearly fluid from his tip before taking it into her mouth.

"Oh, God." Gabriel grunted as his hand tightened around his hard-on. He began to rub himself a little faster, knowing his fantasy wouldn't last long enough, no matter how slow he tried to take it.

Everly had the power to affect him to the core, even if she didn't realize it.

His subconscious mind took note of what felt best each time he caved to the demands of his body. He'd gotten entirely too good at pleasing himself lately. It didn't take him long at all to get off to any number of daydreams about the woman he was quickly becoming obsessed with.

Gabriel would feel guilty about that later. For now, it only brought him pleasure—intense, searing ecstasy the likes of which he hadn't fully understood possible. No wonder people had been lured into immoral acts in the pursuit of this euphoria. He hated himself, and still he couldn't stop.

Focusing only on the high brought by his lewd thoughts, he shoved the rest aside. There would be plenty of time to repent after he'd released the pressure building steadily in his groin.

He cupped his balls and rolled them between his fingers to soothe the ache there.

It wasn't enough.

Gabriel imagined Everly peeking up from between his legs, pausing only to smile at him before rising up and positioning his cock at the entrance to her body. She would welcome him inside, hold him tightly within her as her pussy began its hot, wet massage…

"Gabriel!" When she shouted his name in surprise, he shuddered.

Oh hell yes. Could he bring her pleasure, too? Simply by joining with her like that?

"Gabriel?" This time she sounded less certain. "Oh, I didn't realize you were home today. Are you—? Oh! Shit! Sorry!"

"Huh?" Gabriel's shuttling hand stuttered in its rhythm as it flew along his shaft. The Everly in his mind was morphing from a sex goddess into his friendly neighborhood manager. One who was now ogling him in total shock.

How could he have forgotten she was coming for Goliath's daily walk? Could some devious part of him have wanted her to find him like this? What kind of savage did that make him? Add it to the list of his sins.

He blinked against the harsh light of the afternoon sun and got an amazing view of her pert ass as she bent over to pet Goliath, settling him after the sharp tone of her shriek. If it had been anyone else intruding in their domain, the dog would have barked his massive head off. But he had a soft spot for Everly, too. Instead of alerting Gabriel to her presence, he only wagged his tail and leaned into her gentle caress.

Holy shit!

If Gabriel had been subtle about things, he probably could have turned over and pretended to be like his worldly, sophisticated neighbors Kent and Christina, or Casey, Jase, and Ian, or even Avi. None of them cared about exposing themselves or their sexuality to anyone who looked. Yet they were good people to their core. Another thing Gabriel was still working on reconciling with the remnants of his twisted ideals.

Instead he thrashed like the fish out of water that he was, trying not to drown himself in his frantic attempt to retrieve his bathing suit or vanish. There was no escaping. He was trapped in the fancy glass box of this lavish penthouse with his shame. Now he'd add mortification to the list of issues plaguing him.

Despite her attempt to preserve his dignity, Everly turned to see what the ruckus was about and caught him sliding down the sand he was dislodging as he flopped and splashed about. His raging boner aimed in her direction. At least she didn't know she'd inspired his very prickly condition.

"Oh my God. Are you okay?" Her beautiful eyes widened when she caught his predicament. Without a second thought, she kicked off her high heels and hiked up her skirt, which definitely did nothing to help the situation.

Her legs. Damn, they were gorgeous.

She dashed to the edge of the pool, then splashed through the water like something out of one of his dirty fantasies. Naturally, he was content to stare like an idiot as water droplets sprayed around her, catching the light and refracting it like the crystal chandeliers inside, dampening the silk of her blouse until it plastered against her and revealed the outline of her bra beneath the thin fabric.

How would he ever erase that image from his memory when they were chilling on his couch, watching one of the many movies he'd missed while cloistered from the rest of normal civilization?

He wouldn't. Didn't even plan to try.

Everly reached his side. She leaned over him, steadying him and lifting his head and shoulders above the surface of the pool. All he could do was open and close his mouth like a beached sea creature gasping for air. Despite his best efforts, his gaze dropped from her concerned face to her voluptuous breasts and rapidly hardening nipples.

Nothing was left to his depraved imagination. Next time he dreamed of her, he'd know exactly what picture to paint in his mind. Her curves made his hands itch to cup them, to see if she would fit there as perfectly as he thought she might.

"Gabriel?" she whispered as her gaze raked his body. It seemed only fair that she view all of him, too, when she crouched down beside him for a closer look. He wondered if she liked what she saw.

"Huh?" A strangled noise left his throat along with the last of his breath.

"I didn't mean to interrupt." She cleared her throat, then shocked him again. "But since I did... Can I help you with that?"

Everly had offered to jack him off in the same cheery tone she used to ask when it would be ideal for her to have the annual fire inspection completed or if he'd had any issues with the new security systems they'd installed following the recent trouble in Casey, Jase, and Ian's place.

It was irresistible to Gabriel.

"Please." He slammed his eyes shut and tried to

pretend he was still only imagining things and that this was totally fine. Totally normal. Not wanton or degenerate in the least to take advantage of her like this.

The instant her lips brushed his, he knew his imagination simply wasn't that good. Compared to the real thing, his fantasies might as well have been black-and-white silent movies instead of a 3D film full of special effects.

He groaned and fused their mouths tighter. His hands lifted from the water to cup the back of her head and keep her close so he could devour her.

Everly didn't complain. She parted her lips and flicked her clever tongue against the corner of his mouth, teasing it open. The attraction that had been buzzing between them for weeks ignited in a flash. It raged through him, turning all his inhibitions to ashes in an instant.

Before he realized it, she had progressed from nibbling on his bottom lip to sucking on his tongue. Her actions instructed him as to what she liked and he mimicked her treatment, making her whimper. His cock surged as it bobbed in the warm water of the pool.

When he wobbled in the shallows, she put her hands on his shoulders. Her nails raked the muscles there, bringing him back to reality, where he was mauling a completely innocent woman who had no idea what she was getting into with no commitment or relationship or acknowledgement of affection behind the action.

It was against everything he'd been taught to believe in.

He couldn't do that to her.

So he wrenched away from her hold. For her own protection. Everly didn't deserve to be tarnished by a man like him.

Off balance, she nearly toppled fully into the pool. The hand she flung out sprayed them both with water that seemed to cool her off. When she rose, shaking dazzling droplets from her hair, she stared at him before looking down at herself. The outline of her areolas were clearly visible to them both. Even the pale pink panties between her legs peeked out from below the skirt she'd bunched around her hips.

The astonishment and alarm that chased each other on her pretty face spurred him into motion. Gabriel dove for the towel he'd left on the pool deck. He unfurled it, then trudged into the gradually deepening water to her side.

He wrapped the plush terrycloth around her, obscuring her from his sight before diving for his lost bathing suit and tugging it up his legs. Of course, it did more to mash his stiff cock than to cover it entirely, but it was better than nothing.

When he looked back, Everly was still staring between his legs. Her expression was unreadable.

"I'm sorry," they said simultaneously.

She continued, "Don't apologize. This is your home. I shouldn't be harassing you like this. Don't tell my boss I practically assaulted you, please? I thought—well, anyway, obviously I thought wrong. I swear it won't happen again. I think you should change the code to your locks. Don't give it to me this time."

Everly turned to leave, most likely about to walk out of his life for good.

Gabriel caught her arm in his wet hand. Drops of water rolled down her tan skin, leaving goose bumps he wanted nothing more than to lick until she heated up properly. "Hey, it's not like that. While *I* may be a sinner,

I'm not about to bring a good woman like you down with me."

"Oh, please. You're more likely to go to hell for leaving me hanging all the time than you would be for throwing me a quick fuck. It's fine if you're just not into me like that." Her lower lip wobbled as she stared out at the gleaming New York City skyline. "I don't think I can do this anymore. Be near you and not have you, I mean."

"I'll always be here for you if you need me." That was an easy promise to make. He cared for her. He just didn't know what to do with those feelings. They were too tangled in his hang-ups to sort them out.

"Not like I want." She shook her head. "That's becoming obvious. The timing is bad. You're not ready for more and I shouldn't make you feel shitty about that. I didn't mean to push—"

"Everly?" There were a lot of things in his life he regretted. He didn't want this to be more fuel for the fire burning him alive. He might not have resolved the issues that had plagued him earlier, making it too hard to go out, but maybe this was a sign. He could work on getting one critical aspect of his life in order, at least.

"Hmm?" She peeked over her shoulder, her face partially obscured by a veil of wavy hair, slightly less perfect than usual where it had gotten wet. A flash of running his fingers through it—brushing out the tangles, soothing her for once—inspired him.

Gabriel took a huge gulp of air, then asked, "Will you come over for dinner? I'm an idiot and I have no idea what I'm doing here. But if you really want to see if there's something between us, let's try to do this right. Civilized. Proper. Let me cook for you so we can talk."

God knew he had enough cash to take her to the

fanciest restaurant in the entire city or, hell, even charter a private jet to take them to Paris for a romantic night out. But he couldn't speak as openly with her in a restaurant as he could in his home.

Helping her understand how ruined he was inside and why was something he'd been dying to do for a while now. Would what he had to say finally chase her away?

It'd probably be for the best if it did.

So why did that thought scare him more than leaving his old life behind had?

Either way, it was up to her now. It was time he came clean and let her decide where they went from here.

Everly wrung her hands as she considered his invitation. It actually made him feel less like shit that she hesitated long enough to really think it over before saying, "I'd like that."

"Your shift is over at six, right?"

She nodded.

"I'll have dinner ready," he promised.

"Thank you. I have a feeling I'm going to be hungry as hell." She licked her lips, as if swiping the lingering taste of him into her mouth.

Christ!

Before he could figure out how to respond, she finished drying herself off, straightened her skirt, and collected her shoes. Everly gave Goliath a pat on the head before disappearing through the penthouse.

Gabriel tried not to stare at her ass.

He failed at that, too. Damn him.

2

Everly should be doing her damn job. Instead, she ignored the financial reports open on her computer and spun her chair around. She fluffed her hair and checked her reflection in the enormous window for the 4,723rd time since locking herself in her office after her encounter with Gabriel earlier that afternoon. She was pretty sure no one else could tell how utterly he'd wrecked her with a single kiss.

Okay, a kiss where he'd been gloriously naked and aroused. But still... It wasn't as if she was some blushing schoolgirl. She knew what to do with a man and a cock— even one as impressive as Gabriel's. It was the other, more complicated, *emotional* aspects of their relationship she had no idea how to deal with.

Her eyes glazed over as she internally debated between jumping him and only going upstairs later to tell him that she shouldn't—no, *couldn't*—risk her career by getting entangled with him. *Too late*, she chastised herself. She'd been hooked on him since the moment they met.

Trying to save him from himself had become one of her favorite pastimes.

Maybe tonight he'd finally open up so she could figure out how to help him heal.

If she could make any sort of positive difference in his life, it would be worth the repercussions if something blew up at work. Not that she was going to let their personal relationship interfere with her professional life. No one had to know. It wasn't technically against any rules if they dated.

Movement outside caught her attention, temporarily distracting her from her obsession with Gabriel. Though the higher floors of Beekman Place were reserved for luxury apartments that came with steep price tags, she thought her view on the ground floor was stunning all the same. She loved the whiz of traffic going by and bustling people parading to and from work, the park, or wherever it was they were in such a hurry to reach. The city would always be her happy place. It was full of variety, new experiences, and never got dull. After landing her dream job straight out of Cornell University's hospitality management program, she'd thought she had everything she could ever want.

And then she'd met Gabriel.

Hanging out with him had given her something other than work to look forward to for the past few months. Sure, she'd used taking extra good care of Goliath—their resident hero—as a bit of an excuse to see his owner more. But who could blame her?

Truth was, she was fascinated with the rogue priest who'd moved in and taken over her imagination. What had caused him to forsake everything he'd dedicated his life to? How could someone so indoctrinated in a way of thinking suddenly change their mind?

It took a strong person to wake up and toss away everything they thought they knew for new ideals. Look at politics. Despite endless debate and attempts at persuasion, not many people ever reconsidered their positions, preferring to tell the other side why they were wrong rather than listen to what might have been sound arguments.

Gabriel had done more than that. For reasons he'd never shared with her, he'd embraced dissent and weighed the evidence logically, breaking from everything he'd ever known. Yet he seemed fragile at times, and utterly lost. Out of place.

Selfless, funny, and tortured, he'd made her want to smother him in hugs and make him feel welcome from the moment she'd met him. Today she'd done a lot more than that. Hopefully she hadn't shoved him away in the process of trying to wrap herself tight enough around him to block out his haunting past.

She was about to find out for sure.

Her clock ticked over to six. Despite how long the afternoon had dragged on, suddenly she wasn't sure she could do this. What if this didn't go well?

Everly wasn't ready to lose contact with her favorite resident.

She stood up, adjusted her skirt, then locked her office door before heading to the exclusive elevator used by the owners of the six penthouses at the very pinnacle of Beekman Place. She'd gotten to know each one of them personally and even considered a few of them—like Gabriel, and Casey, who lived next door to him—solid friends.

She prided herself in running the entire building like a well-oiled machine. So what would she do if Gabriel decided to complain about her to her boss? Maybe she should turn around and call him to let him know she'd delegate the handling of his account to her assistant from now on.

She definitely should.

But she didn't.

Couldn't.

Whether he knew it or not, Gabriel needed her. Day after day, he grew more gaunt, more troubled and tense. Soon he was going to spiral out of control. He had to vent or he'd zoom off the top of this skyscraper in loop-the-loops like a balloon that had sprung a leak before plummeting to the ground more than a hundred stories below.

The thought made her clap her hand over her cramping guts.

It wasn't the first time she'd worried for him. Had serious concerns. *That* was why she wasn't running away when every bit of professionalism in her was screaming at her to turn around and go home.

With shaking fingers, she lifted her hand and knocked lightly on his front door despite the fact that she had a master code to every unit in the building.

Goliath didn't even bark. While the soundproofing was plenty good enough for humans, he'd come to know her footsteps or something. He never made a peep when she visited anymore, yet he was always right there waiting. This time was no exception.

Gabriel opened the door. She barely had time to register the tight smile on his face before Goliath gave her a much warmer welcome. He nearly knocked her over when he turned circles around her ankles, whacking her repeatedly with his massive, fluffy tail while he gave her hands extra-sloppy kisses with his ginormous tongue.

"Easy, boy." Gabriel kept the dog from jumping up. Though Goliath would never intentionally hurt her, he sometimes seemed to think he was a tiny puppy or a toy breed that would fit in a purse. It would be easy for him to knock her off balance in her heels. "You have to back off if you want her to come inside. Goliath, sit."

The dog obeyed instantly, though his eyes still shone with the desire to smother her with endless love and affection. If only his owner would do the same—they could skip dinner and go straight to decadent dessert.

Everly petted the dog, but out of the corner of her eyes she studied Gabriel. Despite the fact that he wasn't panting like the dog, she still had his rapt attention.

"Hungry?" he asked.

"Starving." Just not for food. Something had to give or she was going to need to buy stock in her favorite vibrator company. She'd already gone through two since he'd moved in.

Gabriel grinned. It was obvious they had a lot in common. Taking care of others was something they both enjoyed. He rested his hand on her elbow and guided her across the shiny, and slick, marble floor to the formal dining room.

The grand table could easily seat a dozen people. However, he'd only set two places. One was at the head of the table, and the seat right next to it around the corner had a full service of plates, utensils, and linens prepared. A fresh floral arrangement sat nearby, surrounded by burning candles. It seemed he'd even dipped into the temperature- and humidity-controlled wine room to make their evening special. A bottle sat open, the deep burgundy liquid decanting between two elegant glasses.

"Sit and I'll bring the food." He held her chair, then scooted it in so she was comfortable. Oddly so considering she could never have dreamed of affording this place. It hadn't been her goal to keep moving up, like their friend Casey had dreamed of since she was a little girl. Everly was content with the life she'd made for herself.

But this wasn't bad either.

She sat at the table, twirling a fine linen napkin between her fingers while Gabriel carted out enough dishes to feed the entire top floor of the building Thanksgiving dinner. It felt strange to have someone waiting on her, though it seemed normal for Gabriel.

It was easy to forget the purpose behind the meal. It could have been any of the nights she'd spent in the more casual living area, introducing him to the great TV shows he'd missed over the past two decades. For a while, she let them pretend and get settled into their quasi-familiar routines. Not for too long though. Neither of them enjoyed conflict. It would be too easy to ignore the dissonance underlying their civil display.

It would be cowardly not to delve deeper when he'd finally given her a tiny crack in his shields to slip through. She gathered her nerve.

"I'm not sure where to begin this discussion." Everly concentrated on spearing the next ravioli on her fork before taking a large gulp of the best wine she'd ever tasted. The awkward pause that followed her declaration sucked. In all the evenings they'd spent together recently, conversation had never been hard to come by.

"Me either." He shrugged and chewed for a long time before swallowing, as if it was difficult to choke down the amazing food he'd prepared. "You know, I heard a hell of a lot of confessions in my time as a priest. I'm not sure I ever realized how much courage it took people to share their secrets with me. At least they had the shadows of the stall to hide in and the screen between us so they didn't have to face me while they unburdened themselves."

"Is that what you plan to do tonight? Tell me your sins?" She squinted at him, unable to truly believe he'd committed any. He was a decent man. She was sure of it. He'd never intentionally hurt someone.

He set his fork and knife down very deliberately, then looked directly into her eyes. "Yes."

3

"Would it help if we turned out the lights and hid under your sheets?" Everly meant it as a joke. The suggestion fell flat. Probably because both of them were imagining much better ways to spend a night in bed together.

He chuckled. "Pretty sure that would only make things harder."

If by *things* he meant his cock, she thought silently. She was down for that. Judging by his reaction to her solicitation in the pool, he might not be.

Still, he called out to the home automation interface and had it dim the overhead lights so the only glow in the room came from the candles he'd lit.

It seemed oddly intimate and intense. Deep shadows flickered over half of his face, making her think of a man stuck in purgatory, caught between right and wrong. Curiosity was killing her since she only knew one side of him.

She blurted, "Why did you leave the church? Every time you've talked about your life before, it sounds like you enjoyed helping people and were devoted to your beliefs. What could make a man like you turn your back on that?"

It was the question that had been plaguing her for months. If he could bail on such a lofty calling, would he ever be capable of being faithful to anything?

"Technically, they kicked me out. Excommunicated me, to be exact. It was more of a formality. They knew I was leaving and had to make it seem like it was their decision to keep everyone left behind in line. I couldn't stay after I realized everything I believed in had been a lie." His gorgeous lips, which usually smiled so easily, curled into a sneer. "They made me think I was saving souls. That the organization was doing the most good of any on the planet. Really, though, it's just another greedy machine. At the top it's all about politics, wealth, and power. Little people be damned. They'll say or do anything so long as it keeps blind faith and devotion to the religion growing. That's not what I signed up for."

Everly choked down a bite of her bread. Though delicious, it suddenly seemed hard to stomach. What could make someone as positive and uplifting as Gabriel so bitter? It was a question she hadn't found the courage to ask him even after they started hanging out more and more.

"What did they do to you?" She laid her hands flat on the table so she wouldn't be tempted to pick up her knife and start stabbing people. It had to be bad to push him so far away from everything he'd ever believed in.

"They asked me to turn a blind eye to pure evil. To allow it to fester and poison innocent young people." He threw his napkin onto his plate in a ball, his appetite clearly demolished.

"That doesn't sound like your style," she said cautiously, hoping he wouldn't stop there.

Gabriel scrubbed his hands over his face, knuckling his eyes as if trying to erase a memory. Something he'd seen. "I couldn't have lived with myself if I didn't try to stop it."

"What exactly are you talking about?" She desperately wanted to reach out, to hold his hand and comfort him. The way he curled in on himself made her fairly certain he wouldn't welcome her touch right then.

When he dropped his fists and stared at her, she couldn't avoid the agony in his gaze. "I discovered a priest abusing a child. Somehow I managed not to rip him apart with my bare hands on sight. It was the first time in my life I'd ever considered violence even for a moment. Instead, I snapped a few pictures with my cell phone. Then I backed up and made a huge racket coming down the hall, and claimed to need help moving some seats around, to get the kid out of there. I wanted to help him, but I didn't know how. I tried to talk to him, but he got freaked out that I was going to use what I'd seen against him, maybe to do the same thing. He ran into the night and I still don't know what happened to him, because after that everything fell apart."

There were so many things Everly wanted to say, but none of them seemed right or helpful. Instead, she listened to him as her stomach rolled and her heart broke for Gabriel and the victim he obviously hadn't been able to save.

"I immediately reported what I'd seen to the bishop. And..." Gabriel swallowed hard, shaking his head in disbelief. His eyes were glazed, as if he were there in his mind, reliving the experience. "He asked for my phone, to see the pictures for himself. When I handed it to him, he deleted the evidence and ordered me to keep silent. I was stunned. Of course I'd heard the stories. There are too many to discount. Still, I thought *my* parish was different. They weren't. Aren't."

Son of a bitch. Everly was glad they hadn't eaten more. Otherwise she might have been sick at the thought. "Oh, Gabriel. I'm so sorry. Of course you left. Of course you would."

"There had been other things bothering me for a while. Hypocrisies that I reasoned away and doubts that kept creeping in. But *that*...there was no going back from that." Gabriel threw his head back. "Even then I still didn't understand what kind of establishment I belonged to. Until I got back to my room to pack and realized people were giving me odd looks, refusing to speak to me. I found out later that rumors began to circulate about how *I* had been the one found committing those horrible crimes."

"No one would believe that of you, Gabriel. No one who really knew you." She shook her head. "I wouldn't."

"You don't understand what it's like. When you're that deep into any belief system, you don't question what you're told. I wasn't staying anyway, but they made sure everyone I'd ever known or cared for stayed far away from me.

"I didn't have anywhere to go. No money. Nothing. I'd been raised in a Catholic orphanage. I guess that's why it took me so long to see what was really happening. It's hard when you're raised to believe something is the ultimate truth, to start seeing the cracks in those beliefs. It's easy to rationalize them away. For a while I had been floundering, but I believed in the greater good and blew off stories of corruption as the one bad apple in the bunch. Until I realized it wasn't one person and it was a system of deception. It's about politics. Power. Money. Keeping people in line more than helping them out. So I left even though I didn't know anything else. I have no skills."

"So how did Mr. Sapriano find you?" She had always enjoyed chatting with the old man who'd owned this place before Gabriel. He'd had so many interesting life experiences. He'd listened to her, never judged, always offered sound advice when she hadn't realized she was looking for it.

"He used to be a parishioner in my church." Gabriel shrugged. "He'd asked me to come out here and perform private services for him after he got too sick to attend. That wasn't something our bishop would consider without a major donation, despite how generous Paulo had already been with them. So I..."

"You came on your own time." Of course he had.

"He'd become a friend through the years. I'd been over here a few times to see his collection of relics. It was actually my discussions with him that started me thinking I might want to take another direction in my life. He encouraged me to see more of the world and broaden my perspective. Lent me a lot of books on various religions and cultures. Did you know he studied all sorts of belief systems? And though he'd been baptized Catholic, he spent more than ten years as a Scientologist at one point in his life."

"Really?" She tipped her head, fascinated.

Gabriel nodded. "He found a lot of value in the introductory courses they offered that led to self-improvement but as he moved up their Bridge to Total

Freedom without making the spiritual gains they'd sold him on, he became disillusioned and left."

"It seems like he really did try just about everything." Everly couldn't imagine searching her whole life for something and never finding it. Then again, maybe that's what she was doing hunting for a partner. If things didn't work out with Gabriel, she'd eventually move on and hope for a connection with someone else. How many times would she have to be disappointed before she gave up on that dream?

"He wanted to believe there was something bigger out there. But I was here with him at the end. He told me that after all his research and travels, he was pretty sure all that mattered was making the most of the time we're given here and now." Gabriel sighed. "Which makes me think, those times he asked me to come here...*he* was really trying to help *me*."

"I wouldn't put it past him. He was clever and a little sneaky like that." Everly smiled for the first time since they'd started this discussion. "I'm so glad you broke the rules for him."

"It was the right thing to do." He lifted his chin and puffed out his chest at that, as if she would argue with him. How long had he had to defend making ethical decisions when they went against the policy of his church?

"Are you still trying to convince yourself? Come on, Gabriel. You're a decent, compassionate, all-around good man." No, a *great* one. But she didn't think he was ready to hear that from her or anyone else. Not when he'd been brainwashed otherwise. The emotional scars were so deep she didn't know if he'd ever be able to erase them fully.

"You sound like Paulo."

"Well, he was smart. And generous. And a great judge of character." Everly shrugged.

"I believe that. He used to rave about you all the time." Gabriel smiled and reached beside his calf to ruffle the dog's fur. "Once he became confined to his wheelchair, he really appreciated how you helped him take care of Goliath. You know he dreaded having to send this guy away."

She nodded. "He was also terrified of dying alone. Goliath was his only true companion. Until you moved in and took care of them both."

"The truth is...he really was looking after me. When I came to tell him I had been excommunicated and that I wouldn't be able to carry out my duties with him, he offered me a position here. I told him I'd lost my faith. He still didn't care. He made me feel useful, and maybe that made it bearable for him to finally ask for so much help himself. The truth is, he was doing it to save me. I'm not an idiot. I know that. He could have hired a hundred helpers more qualified than me both as a nurse and as a spiritual advisor. I suck at both."

"The fact that he left you his entire fortune, including this place, tells me that you were far more than hired help to him. You were like a son. Someone he felt deserving of his life's work." How could Gabriel not see that?

"Or I just happened to be in the right place at the right time." He shook his head, looking off to the side, out of the floor-to-ceiling glass that allowed a panoramic view of the city spread out below them. "I'm grateful for everything I have today. Especially the time I've had to start finding myself again and figuring out how to actually do what I thought I was accomplishing before—helping people. But damn, it's lonely up here."

"You're not alone tonight," Everly promised, leaning toward him in the candlelight.

"After everything I told you about how I blindly supported a corrupt organization that has ruined countless lives, about how fucked up I am inside over it, you'd still take a chance on me?" He held his hands up, palms out, as if he simply couldn't understand.

"Hell yes."

He swallowed hard, rested his fists on the table, and mumbled, "I have no idea how to do this, Everly. I...uh... I've never been with a woman."

"You're a virgin?" Why the hell hadn't she considered that? "I mean... Of course you are. Vow of celibacy and all that. Right? Wow."

Holy fucking shit.

Gabriel didn't say anything. He just let his admission sink in, all while staring at her as if she was twice as delicious as the meal he'd prepared for them.

So why wasn't he whipping his arm across the table, sending crystal and silver smashing to the floor so he could ravage her right there in the middle of the dining room? She'd made it obvious that she'd be happy to let him feast on her.

Everly asked, "Do you still want to be? Are you holding on to your vows even though you're not officially a priest anymore? Or maybe you're waiting to be married?"

"I don't believe in that stuff anymore." He shook his head.

Thank God. Everly nodded. "Then what's the problem? Are you gay?"

"What?" He squinted. "No, I don't think so. I mean, not that I have a problem with that either. Yet another reason I couldn't belong to an organization that vilified decent people, shamed them, for loving another human being. That wasn't what I thought I'd signed up for."

"Okay." She nibbled her lip. "Then why? You're rich as fuck, sexy, and available. You could have hooked up with half the city by now if you'd wanted to."

"Didn't appeal." He shrugged. "Maybe I'm still too screwed up inside. Lost."

"You're not confused, Gabriel. You're *tormented*. Deep down you know what you want, but I think you feel guilty about it. If you're attracted to me and would like to experiment...there's nothing wrong with that. I want you, too. A hell of a lot."

"You don't know how many times I've dreamt of hearing you say that." He groaned.

Everly bolted to her feet, ignoring the scrape of her chair on the expensive flooring, afraid that if she didn't seize the moment it might slip away from them like all the near misses they'd had in their shared evenings these past few months.

She rounded the corner of the table and stood beside Gabriel. Holding her hand out to him, she said, "Let me show you what you've been missing."

4

———

Everly tried her best not to be distracted by their opulent surroundings as they crossed the main living area to the owner's suite. It was one thing to admire the high-end finishes and impeccable interior design while doing a safety walkthrough and entirely something else when she actually occupied the space as part of her regular life.

During the entire trek to the master bedroom, which had a killer view of Manhattan, Gabriel held her hand. She promised herself she'd take in the epic skyline later. While it glowed with the burnt orange and pinks of the sunset in progress, it would be even more spectacular when the field of infinite lights below began to look like a universe of stars twinkling furiously in the night.

When they reached the side of the enormous bed—carved from some exotic wood, with a tufted leather headboard—Gabriel faced her and took her other hand in his. He brushed his thumbs over her fingers, melting her heart just a little bit more.

She wasn't prepared for how much he made her feel in addition to how badly she wanted to seduce him. He raised her knuckles to his lips and kissed them softly. Without saying a word, he made her certain he respected her and trusted her to make this great for them both.

"Don't worry. I promise it's going to be amazing." Everly smiled up at him, then took advantage of her tall heels. She craned her neck, he leaned in as if he couldn't resist, and then their lips were brushing across each other's again.

This time it was more subtle, less flashy, than this afternoon's venting of pent-up passion. She'd bet Gabriel would become a damn fine kisser. The kind of guy she could snuggle and make out with for hours before giving in to a round of sweet, slow sex that would unravel her thread by thread.

Someday soon. After he'd had some practice.

Tonight would be something else entirely.

She sighed and pulled back before unbuttoning his perfectly pressed shirt. The aqua blue made his eyes stand out. It was also an interesting contrast. Gabriel was the single most humble person she knew, standing here in a fancy shirt he'd probably only ever worn this once, for her, in the middle of a modern-day palace he hadn't asked to rule.

His dirty blond hair was longer now, along with his beard. She liked to think of him as a hipster priest. It was probably wrong for that thought to turn her on, but hey, she'd never claimed to be a saint.

As she admired each inch of his defined chest and abs, she placed a kiss over the parts of him he allowed her to reveal. He stared, transfixed, as she worshiped his body. And she didn't plan to stop with an act as simple as that.

Before she could continue her deliberately slow stripping, afraid of spooking him, Gabriel flew into action. He unbuckled his belt. A few flicks of his fingers were all it took to unbutton and unzip his pants. They dropped around his ankles a moment later.

She licked her lips when she realized there was nothing else between her and his already erect cock. Damn. It would have been impossible not to tease him, just a little, about how eager he was after he'd separated them so savagely earlier. "Commando?"

"A habit." He shrugged.

"Are you telling me you were free-balling it beneath your priest robes?" Everly wondered if she'd go to hell if she asked him to dress up for her once while they got it on... Thoughts for another time.

"Maybe I was just as perverted as the rest." His face clouded over.

Oh no, she wasn't going to let his past ruin their future. Or at least not their present.

This was going down tonight. *She* was going down. That would guarantee he thought of nothing but her and what her mouth could do to him.

"Get up on the bed."

"Shouldn't I undress you first?" His hand hovered over her blouse, waiting for her explicit permission to remove her shirt.

Everly didn't give it. She preferred to put on a show for him.

"Just lay back and enjoy." She had never felt this confident in bed before. Something about the awe in Gabriel's stare and the trust necessary for him to take this step with her added to her conviction that she was about to introduce him to more pleasure than he'd ever experienced before.

She took her time, slowly rubbing her hands up and down her torso, chest, and neck over her clothes before she began to sway in place. Bit by bit she removed first her blouse, then her skirt, revealing her figure to his inquisitive gaze.

Everly pivoted, flashing her lace-covered ass and the length of her mostly bare back to him. She gathered her hair then let it drop in a silky waterfall that stroked her shoulders. Gabriel muttered a curse that she took as a major compliment.

Reaching behind her, she unclasped her bra. The straps tumbled down her upper arms. She faced him again, dipping the garment bit by bit until her full breasts and nipples were on display.

"You're so beautiful," he whispered.

She wasn't sure when he'd moved, but his hand had returned to his cock, rubbing it slowly and thoroughly, like he had been doing when she'd busted him in the pool. Could it have been her he envisioned as he got himself off?

Tonight he wouldn't have to pretend.

Feeling moisture pooling at her opening, she realized she was torturing herself just as much as him. She slipped a finger beneath the waistband of her panties near each of her hip bones, then walked them down, down, down.

Now wearing only her heels, she stepped from the lace without tripping and breaking her neck. That part of her striptease impressed herself the most.

"Can—?" Gabriel clamped his mouth shut before he could make his request, swallowing hard as if to keep the plea inside.

"What do you want?" she asked. She'd give him damn near anything if it spiraled his pleasure higher.

"Can I smell them?" He grimaced, as if she would ridicule his desire or find his natural curiosity disgusting.

Instead she bent over, giving him a stellar view of her ass, and plucked the lace from the floor. She crawled onto the bed, then held the flimsy material up to his face.

Gabriel buried his nose in the panties and breathed deep of her scent. It seemed only fair since he had driven her crazy with lust for hours. No, months. Now he would know what it felt like to burn with need.

He took the panties from her and balled them into his fist, claiming them as a souvenir of their liaison. Everly figured she was turning him on enough to push him beyond his inhibitions. Her not-so-evil plan was working.

She straddled him where he sat, with his shoulders propped on a mountain of pillows.

Everly paid careful attention to his expression as she lifted her breasts, squishing them together to enhance her cleavage. He gulped.

"Do you want to touch them?" she teased.

He obviously did. His hand shot out and he went straight for her nipples, making Everly flinch at the unexpected rough contact. A shocked yelp escaped her before she could stop it.

Gabriel drew his hand back as if he'd been smacked. "You deserve more than a thirty-year-old guy who doesn't know what the hell he's doing in bed." He clenched his jaw. "Maybe this was a stupid idea. Maybe I should have found someone I don't give a shit about..."

"Hey, look at me." She tipped his chin up, lightly massaging the muscles in his jaw until they relaxed some.

He stared into her eyes.

"It turns me on to know that you're not a man-whore like some of the guys I've dated. To know that this is special to you. That you'll remember tonight for the rest of your life. Because I sure as hell will." Everly kissed his forehead. "It means a lot that you'd choose me. Don't take that away from me."

"Then tell me what to do and how to do it to make it good for you." Gabriel's giving nature could make him one damn fine lover, if only he'd quit stressing and trust his instincts.

Everly took his hand in hers and placed it over her breast. They gasped simultaneously as the tentative contact from his palm drew her nipple into a tight peak. "I'd rather show you."

"Yeah. Okay," he mumbled, his gaze fixated on the spot where he cupped her chest. He began to explore, brushing his thumb over her skin and weighing her breast in his hand. "You're so...soft."

"You should feel my skin against your lips, taste it, smell it."

She didn't have to tell him twice. No sooner had the words left her mouth than he'd surged forward, nuzzling her cleavage. He hummed as he captured one nipple between his lips and began to suckle. His teeth scraped her, making her hiss. Observant and responsive, he adjusted his approach by wrapping his lips around the sharp edges before sucking again.

"Use your tongue, too," she urged, threading her fingers into his hair and guiding him to the place that felt the best.

When he flicked it against her, she twitched. One hand landed on her hip to steady her.

She knew right then that when she unleashed the beast within him, he was going to be the one rocking her world. In addition to being compassionate, generous, and protective, he was fierce. Things were going to keep getting better and better. She could hardly wait.

Everly squeaked when he pressed her back farther, knocking her off balance. Instead of righting herself, she clasped his hand and drew him over her, getting him used to asserting himself. His cock nudged her thigh, making her squirm beneath him.

"Sorry. Didn't mean to..."

"We're going to touch all over. It's not a problem. In fact, why don't you come closer? Rub yourself against me. See what feels good and go with it. Anything is fine as long as we're both enjoying ourselves." She pecked his cheek, then whispered, "Go ahead. Try anything you like."

Gabriel groaned. "Seriously, you don't mind?"

"It's more than that. I *like* watching you enjoy yourself. Remember how you took me out for ice cream every day when toasted marshmallow sundae was the flavor of the month?"

"Oh, yeah. I think I'll offer the owner a million bucks to put it on the menu every day. I loved the way you'd purr and lick your lips after each bite." He rocked his hips so his hard-on glided across her skin. "It damn near killed me."

"Were you imagining me doing those things while in bed with you?" She wondered because she'd been wishing they'd done more than shared a sweet treat on those steamy summer nights.

"Yes." He winced. "It wasn't the only reason I wanted to spend time with you, but it was one hell of a bonus."

"Well, now's my chance for turnabout. I'm going to watch you devour me."

"Seems fair." He smiled wide and slow. "Okay."

Gabriel got to his knees between her thighs. He ran his hands over her breasts again, then down her sides and finally over her belly. He stroked her until his heavy cock pulsed against her mound. If he'd shoved inside and rode her furiously, she wouldn't have minded.

Tonight was all about him.

Instead, he took his shaft in hand and tapped it against her, slapping her lightly. The dull thud of his thick flesh and the accompanying shimmer left on her body from his precome had her arching up to meet him.

"Is it okay if I touch you here?" He put his hand lightly over her mound.

"Anywhere you want." She smiled, secretly thrilled that he'd asked. When compared to more experienced guys, it was nice to be with someone who respected her so completely, revered her body and accepted her choices.

"You don't only have to touch me with your hands. Feel free to use your lips, your cheek..." She intentionally scanned from his intense stare to his chest, then lower. "Your cock. Whatever feels best."

He didn't hesitate. With a soft growl, he leapt into motion, startling a squeak from her. Gabriel crouched over her, one foot planted near each of her hips. His knees dented the mattress beside her upper arms, effectively trapping her.

Being at his mercy wasn't a hardship.

She winked up at him when he hovered, the heavy weight of his erection dragging his dick downward until the tip tucked between her breasts.

He fisted himself and began to test different

sensations. First he tapped the head of his cock against her nipple, which made both of them jerk and groan. Then he drew light circles around it, using the motion to spread silky fluid on the delicate skin, easing his passage.

Gabriel seemed to be getting really into it. His abdomen flexed hard from time to time with the instinctive urge to thrust. His eyelids drooped into a sexy, slumberous gaze. Veins appeared on the sides of his neck, proving how desperately he attempted to hold back.

Fuck that.

She wasn't about to let him half-ass his very first orgasm with a woman. Transforming into every man's fantasy fuck and allowing him to be greedy, at least for tonight, was more what she had in mind.

So she reached up, beneath his groin, and cupped her breasts. She plumped them, squishing them together enough to maximize her cleavage before she asked, "Want to fuck them?"

"Is that a thing? Really?" His eyes dilated.

"You need to watch more porn, Gabriel." She grinned. "Hell yes. That's *definitely* a thing."

"It sounds like I'll need you to give me a few site recommendations later." He shook his head. "I'm sorry I—"

"No more apologizing." She distracted him from his self-consciousness by shimmying her breasts. "Get in here."

He didn't say anything else, either to accept or refuse her invitation. Instead, he used two fingers at the base of his cock to point it down, then poked it into her cleavage.

"Try going from the bottom up, along my breastbone." She lifted her torso to align him better with the tunnel she'd made for him to drill into.

His hum sent shivers down her spine as he pushed into the space, molding her breasts around him. Unfortunately, he only made it an inch or two before lurching to a stop. Gabriel withdrew, then tried again with similar results.

Too dry. Damn.

Everly doubted he had lube hanging around, so she improvised. "Hang on, let me get you wet first."

He backed up as if she was going to leave the bed and find some water.

Before he could get too far away, she grabbed his ass and tugged him back. This time she craned her neck upward and opened her mouth. His cock slipped between her lips as if it had been dying to be there all along.

"Oh, God. Yes. Fuck!" Gabriel buried a fist in her hair, tugging her deeper onto his shaft. "Do more of that."

Everly chuckled around him, wanting to save a full-on blowjob for later, after he'd gotten his fill of more simple pleasures. Between his lunges and her laughter, he stabbed a little too deep. She choked. Coughing around him led to nearly gagging.

Only then did Gabriel's eyes open enough for him to realize he was nearly suffocating her with his dick. He withdrew immediately, cradling her head and helping her ease to the side. "Are you okay? Everly? Damn, I'm s—"

She cleared her throat loud enough to drown out his unnecessary apology. "It happens. You're a lot for a girl to handle. No problem. But I'd rather you finish what you started this time around. I think you're plenty wet enough now to try it before we advance to more complicated maneuvers."

Gabriel looked at his glistening cock, her puffy lips, then the valley between her breasts, as if he couldn't decide which to ravish first. Prominent veins surrounded his shaft. The flesh had a deeper mauve cast to it now than it had before. The man needed some relief.

"You're sure you're all right?" He paused, though his hand wandered between his legs to cup his balls as he monitored her for signs of distress.

"Positive. I'll be even better when you get back over here." She wasn't quite sure where she found the inspiration for her dirty talk, but it was fun to watch his jaw tic as she said bold and nasty things. "Come on, Gabriel, fuck my tits. You know you want to."

"I do." He adjusted his stance, then speared into the tunnel she created for his shaft. Slick from her saliva, his cock plunged in far enough that the tip popped out the top side of her breasts.

Everly rewarded his enthusiasm by licking it just before it disappeared for the return journey. It wasn't long before it reappeared and she repeated the action.

Gabriel tipped forward, planting one forearm on the bed over her head. He began to drive into her softness repeatedly. No encouragement needed.

It only took a few strokes before his stride hitched. It surprised her when his cock twitched between her breasts and a spurt of hot seed blasted up onto her neck. She should have realized it would catch him just as unawares.

Gabriel shouted. He tried to withdraw. It was too late. His body had waited a lifetime to find relief. He jerked. Come poured from his cock. It sprayed over her neck and collarbones before he pulled out far enough to glaze her breasts with the rest of his epic release.

He grunted repeatedly, as if each pulse of his climax and the resulting pump of come that decorated her was pulled straight from his soul.

The entire time he emptied himself he stared, fascinated, at the mess he made of her.

Everly loved every bit of the show he put on, losing himself completely in his ecstasy, which was why she noticed the instant his bliss turned into self-recrimination.

5

"**D**amn it. Shit, I'm sorry." Gabriel tipped his head back. He stared heavenward as he attempted to catch his breath.

Everly loved seeing him completely unraveled. By her. For her.

"It's fine." She smirked up at him where he crouched over her as she massaged his ass, which still clenched rhythmically while his body rode the lingering waves of his orgasm. "It turns me on to know you're so into me and what we're doing together."

"We barely took our clothes off before I ruined the fun." He dropped down beside her, grabbed his shirt, and began to clean the proof of his epic release from her chest.

"Shhh." She leaned forward and kissed him to keep him from actually snuffing out her enjoyment with his self-flagellation. "There's plenty more trouble we can get into."

He hesitated, glancing at his softening cock before meeting her gaze once again. "You'll show me how to please you...even now?"

"Of course." She winked. "And I'm pretty sure I can put you back in the game if you'll let me."

He groaned, then squeezed his dick. It seemed the mere thought had already started to turn things around. Before she could direct him, he reached out and resumed his examination of her body. Goose bumps broke out along her arms and her spine arched, pushing her pelvis up toward his tentative touches.

"That feels good?" he asked.

"Very." She bit her lip, then said, "Use your fingers. Play with my pussy."

Gabriel yanked her thighs apart in one swift motion that caught her off guard. Him, too, by the look on his face. Something primitive and instinctual engaged then. He cupped her pussy with the base of his palm over her clit. His fingers naturally aligned with her slit.

He began to pet her. Proving he'd paid attention earlier, when she'd helped him ease between her breasts, he spread her arousal over her flesh until it was slick. His fingers glided across her sensitive skin.

"You're even softer here. Smooth and satiny." He hummed as the tip of his finger delved deeper between her folds. She spread her legs as wide as his nearness would allow. When he saw her responding, he growled low in his throat. Being at his mercy would be incredible.

One day she hoped she got to experience that side of him more fully.

Gabriel surprised her when he lifted his hand, making her whimper at the loss. Until she realized what he was doing. He stuck out the tip of his tongue and stole his first taste of her from his index finger. He hummed and put his finger in his mouth, sucking it clean.

"It's better straight from the source," she promised.

"You want me to put my mouth on you?" He hesitated, as if he hadn't considered the possibility before. Only for a moment, though, until he practically torpedoed between her legs. His enthusiasm ramped up her arousal even more. She speared her fingers into his hair and helped guide him to her core.

Just like he had with his hand, he licked tentatively at first. The initial contact of his tongue with her pussy sent a jolt of desire straight up her spine. She shrieked his name.

Gabriel froze, his gaze flying to hers.

"It was a good scream." She was rapidly losing the ability to speak. Or think clearly, for that matter. "More."

She grunted when he returned with a vengeance, burying his face between her legs as hungrily as he had when he'd sniffed her underwear earlier. He devoured her as if she was a quickly melting ice cream cone. Except each of his laps only produced more cream for him to enjoy.

Without instruction, he added his fingers, spreading her apart so that he could sip every last drop from her as he pushed her closer to the edge of her own orgasm. When his hand slipped in her arousal, his finger nudged her opening.

"Yes. Fuck." She bucked toward him, wedging the digit a little deeper. "Put it inside me, Gabriel."

He pressed lightly, not making much progress. She was clenched tight at just the thought of his initial invasion. "Are you sure this isn't going to hurt you? You seem so tight. Too small."

"I swear." She forced herself to relax as much as possible. "It hurts being empty when I need you so bad. Do it. Please?"

The man he was couldn't resist helping someone out if he had the power to do so. Gabriel stopped breathing as he wormed his finger inside her bit by bit. "You're so damn hot."

"Horny," she corrected. "More."

He leaned back only far enough that he could study her pussy as he fed it another finger, and then another. Once he'd stretched her open, he began to stroke her from the inside as if he couldn't get enough of how she felt. She shifted, helping him begin to withdraw and penetrate in a repetitive motion that was guaranteed to shatter her sooner rather than later.

"Good. Now suck my clit." She threw her head back as he did as instructed. Her pussy clamped down on his hand, trapping it inside her. "If you keep doing that, just like that, you're going to make me come."

He moaned, as if he might be getting off on her pleasure. Hopefully he would hang on. Although, if he lost control and came on the sheets, she'd take it as a challenge to get him hard again. No fucking way was she going home tonight before ensuring he lost his virginity.

His cock would be inside her soon, doing more than his still slightly clumsy fingers were right then.

That thought alone was all it took.

Everly screamed his name. Her heels drummed on the mattress as she flew apart. She ground her pussy on his face as he did his best to keep up. He followed her erratic motions, never letting up on the suction that extended her bliss or allowing her pussy to squeeze his fingers out until her legs turned noodley and her knees fell apart from where they'd been clasping his ribs.

"That was incredible, Everly. I can't wait to feel that on

my dick." Gabriel grunted. "I get why guys' hearts give out in bed. I'm not sure I'll be able to take it."

Usually Everly would be down for proving him wrong. Immediately. But he'd managed to wring one hell of an orgasm from her. She needed a second to catch her breath.

Besides, she wanted to make his first time worthy of waiting practically forever. And she knew just the thing to make it unforgettable.

"In a little while. First, let me show you just how good it feels to have someone's mouth on you." She raked her fingers down his abs, letting her nails scratch him softly. He hissed. His cock twitched before he reclined on the enormous bed. He could have been a king or a god for how powerful he looked then.

"Wait." He put his hand on her shoulder as she got into place, snuggled between his powerful legs. "Don't let me come until…"

"Next time you go over, you'll be inside me first. I promise." She needed that, too, for some reason she couldn't quite explain. "Just a little taste. To get you nice and hard."

"I'm already hard, Everly." He waved toward his stiff cock, which did look pretty impressively erect again.

"Nah. I can do better." She grinned, hoping he knew she wasn't entirely serious. Although, she did want him desperate so that he couldn't think too much when the time came. She craved the wild side of him she could sense carefully wrapped up beneath his calm, steady exterior.

It was time to start becoming the man he had always been meant to be, before people had twisted him up and skewed his perceptions.

Everly started slow at first, teasing him with the flat of her tongue, getting him good and wet. She made sure to stimulate every bit of his cock, from the base to the tip, before actually letting him slip between her lips and fill her mouth.

"Everly, wait. I'm not sure I can... Fuck, that feels too good." His hands fisted in the sheets beside his hips.

She ignored him, certain she could take him to the edge without letting him fall over. Her tongue swiped the underside of his cock even as her cheeks hollowed, sucking him lightly as she slid him slow and deep to the back of her throat. She swallowed around him once, twice, three times, and threw in a light caress of his balls. They tightened in her palm.

He was sweating now, his thighs quivering with the strain of holding back. His shaft might as well have been made of steel.

Gabriel was ready.

She backed off slowly, careful not to rile him further with her retreat.

"Next time I'm going to make you come in my mouth. I'll drink every last drop and love feeling you unravel," she swore. "But tonight I want you inside me. I think you should have a sample of all the things you've been missing."

"Fuck yes," he practically snarled. "Though I can't imagine it could feel better than this."

"Some guys get addicted to blowjobs." She shrugged one shoulder. Maybe it would be his favorite sexy time activity. "I guess there's only one way to find out what you like best, isn't there? It's time, Gabriel."

Despite her best efforts, he balked. "Wait."

Had she pushed him too fast? Too hard? It was fine if

he wasn't ready. Sure, she'd be disappointed, but she understood. She cupped his face in her hands and kissed him lightly. "Are you okay?"

"I'm about to explode." He groaned. "But that's not it. I don't have any protection for you. Never needed condoms. Maybe Ian and Jase or Avi—"

"Don't worry. I've got it covered." She bolted from bed before he could stop her or surface from the haze of lust lying thick over them. After rummaging around in her purse, she found a strip of condoms and sprinted back to Gabriel, setting her own personal best time.

When she dashed into his room, he was idly stroking his cock, keeping himself impossible hard. For her. From the fluid jerks, she figured he'd had a lot of practice handling himself. When he spied her bouncing tits, his fingers tightened their hold on his shaft. Everly practically dove back into bed, brushing his hand aside.

"I've got this," she said with a grin as she took over for him while tearing the condom wrapper with her teeth and her free hand. Wasting no time, she placed the thin latex over the tip of his cock, then rolled the rest down his shaft, sheathing him in it.

A strangled gurgle left his throat when she wandered from the base of his dick to cup his balls. "Everly, you better not. That feels...incredible."

"That's all I want, Gabriel. For you to feel as amazing as possible." She kissed him softly then, crawling closer despite her words. Because she had a feeling once he was buried inside her, he was going to forget all about the teasing she'd done so far.

"If that's true, come here. I want to hold you while we do this." He put his hands beneath her arms and tugged her so that she straddled him. Their torsos met as he wrapped his arms around her and kissed the shit out of her. What he lacked in finesse, he made up for with passion.

His hands roamed the length of her bare back, making her as hungry as he was. Maybe more, because she knew what was ahead for them.

"Are you ready?" she asked him between kisses.

He paused long enough to nod. "Dying to be inside you. You do it. I don't want to hurt you. I mean, if I'm even big enough for that."

"You're plenty blessed." She put her hand on his cheek and smiled. "But nothing about this is going to hurt."

Everly hoped she wasn't wrong about that, because already she knew she'd wandered into dangerous territory. He might have been giving her his body tonight, but he'd taken a piece of her heart without even trying. How could she not fall for him at least a little after this?

Lifting up just enough to stand his cock up and aim it between her legs, she settled the tip at the entrance to her body. That simple contact, poised to be so much more momentarily, was one of her favorite parts of fucking. Intimate and full of anticipation, it made her sigh.

"Jesus, you're pretty when you fuck." He studied her and the effect he had on her. The intensity of his appreciation had her muscles going weak.

Everly sank the barest bit onto his cock.

Gabriel groaned and cursed. His hands flew to her hips, both to steady her and maybe to control her descent. If she did this wrong, she might make him feel more insecure instead of building his confidence in bed.

Then again, taking it slow might be impossible for him, too. He was restless and impatient.

Gabriel's hands wandered to her ass. He clutched her

in his palms, spreading her cheeks. Using his grip, he assisted her motions while she raised and lowered herself above him. He learned her rhythm as he helped impale her on his thick shaft, introducing a little more of his cock to her pussy each time she descended.

Damn, he was so fucking hot without trying. Naturally passionate. How had he suppressed this side of his nature before? It had to have been a major sacrifice. One that he now believed meant nothing.

If only it would be as easy to fix the rest of his wounds as it would be to give him physical relief. Everly hoped this at least gave him a temporary respite from the turmoil he'd endured so far.

She looked up, meeting his reverent gaze as he filled her. Though tonight was supposed to be all about him, suddenly it became about both of them, joined together for the first time.

Riding him like that did incredible things to her own body even as she used it to blow his mind. His muscles rubbed her clit, making her pussy hug him tight within her.

Damn.

She shivered in his arms.

"I'm giving you pleasure?" he whispered.

"So much." She didn't even have to fib. Her toes curled. She planted her hands on his shoulders so that she could pick up the pace. Not only because she thought that's what he would like, but because her body demanded it.

"God, that's incredible." He leaned in and bit her lip, startling her. In a good way. A rush of ecstasy blossomed from the place where he'd nipped her and spread throughout her entire being. She clenched around him, suddenly wondering if she might have to try to outlast Gabriel after all.

He stared at her, fascinated when he absorbed the reverberations of her euphoria. His cock twitched within her, driving the barest bit deeper than before.

It hit just the right spot.

She moaned and threw her head back.

"There?" he asked. "Should I do that again?"

Her guttural moan of assent must have translated to the primitive side of his brain. He did. Again and again and again.

Everly's fingers dug into his shoulders, trying to hold on. It was no use. Being with him like this, seeing the honest emotions—tenderness, lust, homecoming, relief, and satisfaction—pouring off of him as she worked his cock... It was the most erotic thing she'd ever experienced.

She called his name, then broke into a flurry of motion.

Everly practically bounced on his cock, fucking them both furiously as she raced toward orgasm. Holding back no longer mattered, for either of them. They were there, together, about to implode.

She should have realized that he'd get off on giving someone else pleasure. That was so his thing. The best thing she could do for Gabriel was to enjoy the pressure of his cock as it tunneled within her and the heat of his body surrounding her, protecting her, while she took her fill of his.

Staring straight into his gorgeous eyes, she allowed herself to be vulnerable. She let him see everything he did to her and how monumentally he'd changed her life by sharing this with her. Everly refused to blink even when she came apart in his arms.

She called his name, then quaked, embedding him fully inside her as she started to climax.

Just before he joined her, Gabriel roared, then flipped them.

Caught off guard, and in the throes of pleasure, Everly couldn't do more than shudder beneath Gabriel as he pounded into her a few times. Though his motions were somewhat stiff and jerky, the unrefined fucking only served to heighten her peak. Her pussy undulated around him, guaranteeing his demise.

Gabriel shouted her name. He plunged into her hard and deep enough to rattle her teeth. While locked together, he stared straight into her eyes and flooded the condom he wore. His body spasmed a half dozen times before he collapsed on top of her, mumbling God knew what. They flew together while riding the natural high brought on by their shared orgasm.

She clung to him, afraid to let go.

If the first time he'd had sex was the best she'd had in her whole life, what would he be like when he got some practice? She wasn't sure, but she definitely wanted to find out.

Eventually their breathing calmed, her heartbeat slowed, and Gabriel's cock slipped from her body. He sighed and shifted to his back before gathering her to him. Everly gladly snuggled against his side, her arm draped across his torso. He surrounded her with his warmth and strength, holding her close.

"Thank you," he whispered. "*This* is heaven."

6

———

"Was it as good as you imagined?" Everly wondered lazily as she tucked into place against Gabriel.

"It was. This is even better." He hugged her tight, afraid to let go now that he realized what he'd be missing if he did. "I've never spent the night with someone. Would you stay?"

"Mmm, yeah. If you kicked me out right now I'd probably only make it as far as Casey's place. I think I came so hard my bones melted."

Gabriel chuckled. It was nice to know he wasn't the only one wrecked.

He couldn't imagine a better woman to share his first time with than Everly. She'd made him feel comfortable, desirable despite his inexperience. Somehow, he'd even managed to reflect some of the pleasure she'd given him. When he'd felt her lose control and wring him dry, it had been like a beam of light piercing storm clouds. For the first time in a really long time, he'd been oblivious to every impediment to his long-term happiness. Free and overflowing with the peace he used to attribute to the benevolence of some higher power.

Could he learn to find that calm within himself again?

Maybe with Everly's help, he could.

"Can I ask you something?" Her voice roused him from his thoughts. Husky with a hint of sleepy, it sounded sweeter than usual to him. He wouldn't deny her anything right then, or ever, really.

"Of course." He ran his fingers through her hair, nudging stray wisps off her face.

"That wasn't the first time you ever came, was it?"

"Technically I came twice, so no..." He couldn't stop his smile as he recalled the flood of pleasure that'd intoxicated him. Even now he was drunk on rapture.

Her eyes widened. "Seriously?"

"Nah, I'm only teasing. I'm an expert-level masturbator." He shrugged.

Everly snorted at that. "I'd like to see that sometime."

"Seriously, that would get you off? It seems kind of pathetic to me." Gabriel cleared his throat. "In a technical sense, it was also a violation of my vow of celibacy. Another sin to feel guilty about. But if I didn't take care of things when I could, in private, it sometimes led to embarrassing situations. I shared living quarters with a bunch of other men. More than once I woke up to wet underwear after vivid dreams. Dreams that almost scared me with their intensity. When I admitted it, instead of penance, the priest who took my confession told me to take care of myself. For a long time I resisted. Eventually, though, I realized he was right. Except once I started, I couldn't quit doing it."

"Why would you want to? It's only natural. Sexy to think about, too. You wouldn't want to watch me pleasuring myself?" She arched a brow before angling toward him, resting her chin on her fist. "You're the first guy in the history of my dating life to feel that way, if so."

"That's entirely different." He perked up, surprising even himself with his rejuvenating hunger. It was like she'd just offered him dessert after stuffing him with a delicious meal. You made room if you had to. Suddenly, Gabriel thought he might have to. He had a lot of wasted time to make up for. "Would you do that? For me? So I could watch?"

"Of course." She brushed a kiss on his shoulder. But now that it had been unleashed, her curiosity took over. "Was that the only stuff you did before? You never snuck a glimpse at porn or anything?"

"Nah." He shook his head. "You have to understand, it was ingrained in me since birth that these things were evil, or at least impure. Although I started to think for myself somewhere along the way, it's hard to shake something you've been taught all your life, you know? That isn't to say there weren't extracurricular activities going on around me, though. I heard and saw plenty in the showers or bathrooms at night. Shadowy corners...."

"No one ever propositioned you? I find that hard to believe. You're sexy as fuck." She caressed the muscles in his upper arm. "Not like any priest I've ever met before."

"They did." He cleared his throat. "At the end there were a few offers I actually considered. Another reason I knew my time was growing short. The longer I stayed, the more I realized I didn't belong. I was headed down a slippery slope, picking and choosing what parts of the faith to uphold and which rules I could bend. The other stuff I told you about, that was the final straw."

"You know there's nothing wrong with being turned

on by what they wanted to do with you as long as it was consensual, right?" Everly paused, as if choosing her words carefully.

He appreciated her tact. Could she sense this was part of his hesitation to pursue a relationship with her, and the guilt that had been eating him alive?

"Are you attracted to men, too? It's totally fine if you're bisexual." She swallowed hard then. "Or even if you decide that although we enjoyed ourselves tonight, you're gay. I'll support you no matter what."

Gabriel didn't want to build her expectations. New experiences bombarded him daily. It was a lot to take in. Confusing. Besides, he'd learned that unless he kept an open mind and dug deep even when it was uncomfortable, he might spend his whole life living a lie.

"I don't know what I am, Everly." He grew serious then, the stony set of his jaw returning. "I probably shouldn't have done this with you until I know the answers to all those things. I tried to keep my distance from you, but I couldn't. I'm sorry—"

He drew the sheet over his legs and tugged it to his waist.

"Oh no. No fucking way will I let you feel bad about what we shared tonight. Even if it never progresses beyond this, it's been one of the most phenomenal experiences of my life." Everly flung the covers off him, exposing him to her and the rest of the world. "Don't hide."

"You don't deserve to be toyed with." He put his hand over his face and groaned. "I care about you. I meant what I said before, I don't want to hurt you. And I'm pretty damn sure I'm going to. I don't know what the hell I'm doing here, Everly."

"You're fine, Gabriel. You're exploring and I am a willing participant in your research. I know the score. You haven't hidden anything from me." She hesitated for just a second, long enough to catch his attention.

"What are you thinking?" He reached out and squeezed her hand, drawing her attention to him once again.

"I know a guy. Someone who would probably be down for a good time." She hedged, wondering how much to share. "With you or me or..."

"Us?" Gabriel's eyes widened. "Is that what you're saying?"

She nodded. "I kind of might have, you know, had a few threesomes with him before. With other guys...and a couple of women. Nothing serious, though. Fun stuff. *Really* fun."

"What is it with these penthouses?" Gabriel's laugh ricocheted off the giant panels of glass making up two whole walls of the corner room. "Or does everyone in the world like to get it on in groups? Was I *that* sheltered?"

Everly shrugged. "Hey, you never know what goes on in peoples' bedrooms. But the more the merrier, I say."

No wonder she was so sure of herself when it came to intimacy. Gabriel tried not to let that bother him. Suddenly, he felt slightly possessive about Everly despite the fact that he had no claim to her whatsoever.

What the hell was that about?

"If I said I was interested..." He cleared his throat.

"Yeah?" She rubbed up against him as if she was down to fuck some more. The thought alone had him delirious with rejuvenating desire.

"What would that mean for us?" Gabriel took a deep breath, then admitted, "My feelings for you run deeper than what we did here tonight. I think you should know that before we go any further. Before I fuck this up too. You're important to me and I don't want to lose you over sex."

Everly silenced his reservations by reaching up and drawing him to her for a long, lingering kiss. She might have forgotten to answer him entirely except that he knew his eyes were full of questions and doubt.

Reluctantly, they separated long enough to finish their discussion.

"It means that we're going to grow closer, sharing another unforgettable first. And no matter what happens, we'll always have that bond. Gabriel, I respect you for making yourself so vulnerable. For trusting me to help you find your way to the rest of your life."

"Okay." He nodded. "Set it up, please."

"This is going to be so damn hot." Everly attacked him, smothering him with kisses.

After an entire night spent not sleeping, he was pretty sure he wasn't gay. Though he might like other flavors of loving, he enjoyed Everly's brand too much to imagine going without it for an hour, never mind the rest of his life.

They were still awake, catching their breath from another round of lovemaking, when her alarm went off. The sky had grown lighter. Hints of blue, pink, and orange seeped into the darkness. They'd made it through the night. Together.

"Call in sick, Everly." Deception wasn't usually a part of his playbook, but he'd do almost anything to keep her by his side. Forever.

She shook her head and laughed. "Sorry, I'm not a good liar."

"Okay, then. Call in well-fucked." He ran his fingers down her spine and squeezed her ass. "I'll call your boss and request special treatment, if that will help."

"I'm entirely too tempted by that suggestion. You're right, management caters to our exclusive residents. But there's no way I'm letting you make that call. I have time for a shower. A long shower, if you want to join me. After that you're going to have to let me go. Especially if you want me to call my friend. If we're lucky, tonight could be even better than last night."

"So soon?" Gabriel sat up, shifting until his feet rested flat on the floor.

"Haven't you waited long enough to discover these things about yourself?" Everly asked. "I can see that it's killing you. Let's find out exactly what you want together. Nothing you learn will make me think less of you. I care for you unconditionally."

"It's funny," he scoffed. "That's the kind of attitude I thought I'd prescribed to my whole life. But I see it more from you and people around here than I did from the people who pretended to uphold those values. I admire you for how open and giving you are."

Everly looked as if she might start to cry for a moment. Instead, she opted for lightheartedness. "Your time to show me how much you worship me is running out and I know this apartment has one hell of a fancy bathroom. Why don't you show me what those six shower heads are really made for?"

"Good point." Gabriel jumped from bed and scooped her into his arms. "Let's get you clean so we can get dirty all over again."

"Now you're talking."

7

———

Gabriel had considered calling off Everly's wild plan several times an hour, all day long. Yet every time he'd taken his cell phone out to dial her office, he'd stared at it before putting it back in his pocket.

He owed it to her to do this. To try it and see if his curiosity was a product of the environment he'd been part of for so long—one where there wasn't any outlet for his repressed desire than the men surrounding him—or something his subconscious was trying to tell him. He didn't intend to toy with Everly's emotions, so it was better to find out with her than bottle it up and realize later that this had been another mistake. One that would impact her as much as him.

At least that's what he kept telling himself. He still jumped when Everly's signature knock sounded on the door right before she used her code to let herself in as usual. She peeked inside as she called his name.

When he yelled hello, she entered then smiled as he approached the grand entryway from the other end of the adjoining living area. This time she wasn't alone. A tall guy, who wore an excellently tailored suit, trailed behind her. His spiky blond hair and bright green eyes were only outshined by his killer smile. When Everly did something, she really went all the way.

If there was a guy Gabriel could be attracted to, this man was probably the one.

Despite his trepidation, he felt instantly at ease. He should have realized any friend of Everly's would be the kind of person he would get along with, too.

Things could easily have been awkward given the situation.

They weren't.

As if it was an everyday occurrence to be introduced to someone your friend had arranged a hookup with, the guy strode straight to Gabriel. He extended his hand. "Hey, I'm Colton. Everly told me you're trying to figure some shit out. I'm down for some sexy times with you both."

New life goals. Gabriel immediately wanted to be more like that—straightforward, unashamed, confident. Open and ready for new experiences. Bold.

That was attractive.

So he simply stood there and let Colton use their lingering grip to draw him in. He didn't flinch when Colton laid his lips on Gabriel's, then proceeded to kiss the shit out of him. Unlike Everly, he wasn't soft. Or gentle. He took...and gave.

For a few moments Gabriel was too shocked to do more than kiss him back. Their exchange was intense and a little violent. It thrilled him when Colton let him know by example that he didn't have to be careful. He could let loose all the passion inside him. It was so weird, like he was watching himself from outside his body.

Did it feel good? Shit, yes.

Did he want to keep doing it? Not so much.

He'd rather make out with Everly, even if their contact was sweeter and slower than this frantic blast of infatuation and wonder he exchanged with Colton.

As quickly as it had exploded, it fizzled out.

Where kissing Everly impacted both Gabriel's body *and* his soul, this was a pleasure that floated on the surface. Something critical was missing. It only took an instant for him to be certain of that. He blinked a few times, then whispered, "Sorry."

"Well, damn." Colton licked his lips as if he'd like another taste of Gabriel. "I guess this is going to be an early night for me."

"What do you mean?" Everly tipped her head as she studied the men in front of her. "That was hot as hell."

"Your boy isn't into me." Colton brushed the pad of his thumb over Gabriel's swollen mouth, letting him know it was okay. There were no hard feelings. His acceptance restored another sliver of Gabriel's faith in his fellow humans. "Not like he's into you."

"I'm not sure if I should be glad or disappointed, to be honest." Everly chuckled, her voice already full of the husky quality Gabriel had come to associate with her arousal.

Had she been looking forward to this? The last thing he wanted to do was let her down.

"Wait." Gabriel grabbed Colton's sleeve as he turned to go. "Do you want to stay anyway?"

Everly and Colton both asked, "Why?"

"I could use a tutor." Where the hell had that

suggestion come from? Gabriel realized then that some things about himself would always remain the same. He enjoyed caring for others. He got off on bringing people pleasure.

Everly's enjoyment would increase his own, and Colton could coach him. It seemed like something Colton might get off on, too. So why not let him watch? Win-win-win.

"How do you feel about that?" Colton asked Everly. "I'm getting the feeling this isn't like other times we've fooled around. This means something to you. Am I going to mess that up?"

"How do I feel?" Everly released an animalistic sound that had Gabriel half-hard in a flash. "I *feel* really fucking horny. I've been thinking about this all day, and if someone doesn't fuck me soon I'm going to burst into flames."

She reached out and gripped each man by the hand before dragging them toward the nearest guest bedroom. Gabriel wondered if she'd chosen it because it was closer or because she preferred to keep his personal space just for them.

Either way, he approved.

Colton started stripping the second he crossed the threshold. Everly and Gabriel followed his lead. Things were happening so fast he didn't have time to process them. This wasn't like the slow unfolding of his previous encounters with Everly.

This was about scratching an itch.

He did his best to keep up, but he'd be lying if he said he didn't miss the scenic route they had taken before.

"How do you want to do this?" he asked them.

"Why don't you show me what you've got and then I'll

make some suggestions?" Colton smirked as he rubbed his chest and then took his stiffening cock in his hand. He stroked himself idly, waiting for them to agree.

Everly nodded. "I like that plan."

She reached for Gabriel's cock and pumped him a few times until he was good and hard. More than ready, like she had told them she was, too.

"It helps if you get on the bed, babe." Colton shoved her lightly so that she half-flopped, half-tumbled onto the mattress. He crawled on beside her. They both looked at Gabriel.

So he joined them, making Everly bounce as he leapt over her like a hunter falling on its prey. Should he kiss her first? Go down on her like he had the night before?

"Don't make me wait anymore, please." She reached up and drew him to her.

Colton wrapped his fingers around Gabriel's wrist, guiding their hands to Everly's pussy. "I can already tell you it's not a problem, but why don't you check to see how wet she is? If she's turned on enough, you can skip a few steps without making her uncomfortable."

It reassured Gabriel to have someone there who knew what to do, who understood his concerns. He wanted to take what Everly was offering but not at the expense of her comfort or enjoyment.

He prodded her with his index finger. It slipped across her waxed pussy and nudged her clit. She moaned.

Gabriel tried again, this time pressing steadily until his digit poked through the muscles guarding the entrance to her body. They admitted him more freely as he began to stroke her, loving the feel of her on his hand.

"Did you forget what you're doing?" Colton grinned. "Don't get distracted. You have the answer."

Everly was more than prepared for him.

He withdrew his hand and licked her cream from his fingers.

Colton cheered him on. "That's right, get nasty. Show her how much she turns you on. Better yet, give her your cock. Watch her face as you stretch her around your shaft. You've got a nice fat dick—I bet that's going to feel fantastic."

"It does." She winked at Colton.

So Gabriel gave her what she clearly wanted. He levered up on one elbow and reached beneath himself to guide his hard-on to her. With far less caution than he'd used previously, he fit himself to her and pushed.

At first her pussy resisted.

"Back up a little and go at her again." The steady stream of Colton's instructions spurred Gabriel to action. "Work your cock into her. Open her up to you."

Gabriel did as he was told. Soon the tip of his dick was notched in Everly. She gasped as he penetrated her bit by bit.

"That's not a bad sound. Keep going." Colton spoke for her when she had no words.

Everly nodded, though, so Gabriel did until he'd given her every inch he had.

He could have spilled inside her right then, before they'd even really got going. It was tempting. She had the power to affect him that intensely, that fast. So he stopped, locked together with her.

A while passed before Colton chuckled, though it wasn't mean-spirited. "You have to move sometime."

"I don't have a lot of stamina yet." Gabriel cleared his throat as he began to fuck. Truth was, Everly pushed him to the edge of his control within moments. Every single time.

"That'll come with time. Try to distract yourself as you get close. Think of anything other than how hot and tight her pussy is on your cock."

Gabriel grunted. He nearly came on the spot. "Not helping."

Colton laughed. "Sorry about that. Take a break when you need to. Here, pull out."

Though it went against every instinct he had, Gabriel did as directed. He gripped the base of his shaft and left the paradise he'd found between this gorgeous woman's legs.

She whimpered and arched toward him. Leaving her unfulfilled wasn't what he wanted either.

"You have two options..." Colton swallowed hard.

"Yeah?"

"Eat her pussy while you take a time out." He stared at Gabriel, hesitating for the first time since he'd arrived.

"Or?"

"Let me get in there and keep her entertained while you're cooling off a little. If we take turns, we can keep her coming without crossing that line ourselves. We can make this last all night long."

All. Night.

Mind blown.

"What do you want?" Gabriel asked Everly.

He hadn't meant to tease her, but she practically roared, "Someone fuck me. Now!"

"Go ahead." A nod in Colton's direction had the man leaping into action as if he'd been tapped in a tag-team fight. He took a condom from the nightstand, rolled it on, then positioned himself between Everly's creamy thighs.

"It's been a while, huh?" He smiled at her as he fit himself to the opening of her body.

Gabriel stared, fascinated, as he used the tip of his cock to rub the sensitive flesh there while also coating himself in Everly's arousal. Smart.

She seemed to enjoy the glide of his cock over the exterior portions of her pussy. A gasp escaped her reddened lips as she grinned up at Colton. "You're such a jerk. Please, fuck me."

Hearing her beg, even a little, did strange things to Gabriel. Something inside him responded to her plea. Although he knew he'd shoot deep inside her if he penetrated her tight rings of muscle now, he couldn't wait to return to her. To make her want him like that.

The things he was learning—about himself, mostly— were fascinating. Addicting.

"While I'm doing this, you should kiss her," Colton encouraged. It wasn't a spectator sport, after all. "Play with her tits. Rub her clit. Touch her everywhere while I fill her pussy."

As he spoke, Colton pressed inside Everly. He slid in deep and steady until his balls tucked tight against her body.

Damn.

Though it was tough to look away, even for a moment, Gabriel focused on Everly. It shocked him when he realized that although Colton fucked her, her attention was riveted on him. When they exchanged heated looks, her eyes rolled back. She gripped his hand as she flew into an unexpected orgasm.

Colton rode her through it, pulling out when she'd finished quaking. "You're up. Too much more of that and I'm done."

Gabriel gladly took his turn. He pumped into Everly longer this time, lazily as she recovered from the first of many, many peaks they would lift her to.

They traded places so many times, Gabriel should have been dizzy.

He'd never get enough of seeing Everly unravel between them though. Eventually, each round got shorter and shorter. Even switching off wasn't keeping his arousal in check.

Sweat rolled down Colton's brow and his jaw clenched tight each time he thrust into Everly's welcoming body. They hadn't exactly made it all night long, but it was becoming obvious that they'd reached the limits of their bodies.

Everly had stopped responding with coherent replies. Now she relied on gasps, moans, and whimpers to encourage them.

As if he had the same thought, Colton called out to Gabriel. He lifted his head from Everly's chest where he'd been sucking on her tight nipple. "You two are too sexy together. I've got to come."

Everly made a strangled noise Gabriel had begun to associate with an early warning of her impending climax. "Are you going to come, too? Show him how much you appreciate what he's done for us tonight. Make it good for him. Go ahead."

Her eyelids flew open. Her gaze whipped to his then to Colton.

Everly froze, then bucked, nearly dislodging Colton as he ramped up the speed and force of his movements until his cock drilled into her hard enough to make Gabriel wince. She seemed to have no complaints.

With a scream, she climaxed. The rhythmic flexing of

her channel triggered the other man's release as well. He embedded himself in her fully before his ass clenched repeatedly in time to his grunts and curses.

It was surreal to watch his lover share that moment with another man. Except not. Because he could see a difference between the physical relief Colton and Everly gave each other and the outpouring of emotion that amplified her and Gabriel's lust when their bodies did the same thing together.

Colton slid from Everly as he finished. She sighed but held her arms open to Gabriel.

"Are you sure?" he asked. "That looked pretty satisfying. You're so tired." He brushed sweat-dampened hair from her brow as he cuddled her, making sure she knew he was fine if she was done.

"I'm sure." She smiled and lifted her face toward him for a kiss. "I need you. I need this."

Who was he to argue?

Gabriel worked himself inside her one final time for the evening. He started slow, rebuilding her pleasure even as he paced himself for one final wild ride. The motion of his hips felt so natural now, he couldn't believe he had worried about his ability to fuck just a day ago.

It took a while, but before too long, Everly was meeting him thrust for thrust.

She sucked on his tongue, humming around it as he held her close while he plunged into her over and over. Long, liquid glides of his cock through her pussy drove them both insane.

The affection in the stares they exchanged sped the beating of his heart.

Everly touched all of him. Cared for all of him.

Beyond speaking, he hoped she understood that he felt the same for her.

Only her.

With that certainty, Gabriel's cock jerked within her. He couldn't say what possessed him, but he leaned in and bit her neck. Not too hard, just enough so that she knew he planned to claim her, now and forever.

That he was giving all of himself in return.

The instant his teeth latched onto her skin, Everly stiffened. She screamed his name as she unraveled in his arms. The firm massage of her pussy triggered his own orgasm. It drew the come from his balls. He flooded her, only realizing once it was far too late that he'd fucked her bare, with nothing between them.

Everly didn't allow him to retreat. She locked her legs around his waist and dug her heels into his ass. She hugged him with her limbs and her spasming muscles. Her restless hands clutched him, pulling his hair, scratching his back, showing him in every way possible that she had to be connected as tightly as possible to him.

He needed the same.

When Gabriel could think again, he kissed Everly's cheek and slipped from her body.

A noise from beside them startled him. It was Colton, clearing his throat. The man knuckled a drop of moisture from the corner of his eye. It could have been sweat.

"I think it's time for me to head out. You two have this under control on your own. There's a lot of porn on the internet if you need some more tutorials. You don't need me." He smiled somewhat sadly at them. "Maybe someday I'll find what you've got."

Gabriel sat, stunned. He thought back to when Colton

had arrived and how he'd wanted to be more like the man. And now the guy was envying Gabriel.

Holy shit.

He rolled to his back and stared up at the coffered ceiling, thinking hard while Colton got dressed and Everly saw her friend out. In addition to his sated body, his mind settled, finding some peace for the first time in years—since he'd started questioning his faith.

Ironic since he'd swear finding Everly had been some sort of divine intervention.

He must have drifted off because the next thing he knew, daylight was brightening the windows and the splash of the shower was making him have to piss.

It was the first uninterrupted night's sleep he'd had since he'd been kicked out of the church. That had to mean he was getting his life on the right track.

Gabriel stretched and rolled from bed. He finished up in the separate toilet room just as Everly shut off the blow drier and fluffed her hair.

He kissed her good morning and tried not to mess up her makeup too badly. Then he leaned his hip against the counter as she put on the elegant lace bra she'd worn the day before, leaving her ass bare. When she finished, she looked over her shoulder at him and smiled slow and wide. "What? It won't be the first time I've gone without panties."

"You're gorgeous. But that's not what I was thinking about. I just wanted to say thank you." He rested his forehead on hers feeling a spark of unease as she prepared to leave him for the day. She was so damn wonderful. Gorgeous, smart, and kind. He couldn't possibly compete with what she had to give him.

"That's not necessary." She kissed him lightly before

saying, "I'm the one who will benefit from your education. Besides, I had just as much fun as you did. More, I think."

Gabriel's glow soured. It hadn't been amusing to him. It had been serious shit. Life changing. It didn't shock him that the evening hadn't held the same importance to her. It still kind of stung, though.

"But it was a risk, doing this with me. I admire you for taking it so we could see if we were a perfect fit." Unfortunately, they weren't. He was still learning to walk. She flew.

Gabriel separated them and held her at arm's length. A chill crept in through the warmth her presence in his life had brought. "And I promise I'm not going to take advantage of your humility and charity. I should let you go before someone gets hurt or our friendship is ruined."

"What are you talking about, Gabriel?" Her eyes narrowed.

"I know I'm not good enough for you. For anything more than some *fun*, anyway."

Everly flinched. Then she sprang into action. She stomped over to her discarded clothes and began to yank them on.

"What did I say?" He rewound the words that had come out of his mouth but couldn't find anything offensive in them. Only the truth.

"You're throwing what I said in my face and using it as some kind of excuse to blow me off. How stupid do you think I am?" She whirled, glaring at him now. "If you've decided you're not that into me after all, that's fine. I can handle rejection. Just be honest."

"Huh?" He didn't chase after her as she strode for the door because he was too stunned to move. "Everly, hang on. You misunderstood me."

"Did I?" Her voice held a sharpness he'd never heard before. "Because I'm pretty sure you were spouting some bullshit about your worth that was going to piss me off and jeopardize our relationship. *If* that's what we have. Is that what we have, Gabriel?"

The *yes* he craved to shout got stuck in his throat.

"Or are you going to spend the rest of your life so busy kicking yourself that you can't make the best of all these opportunities you've been given?" She propped her hand on her hip.

What felt like the single most amazing thing he'd ever experienced might actually be the most selfish. He tried to consider her first, but apparently he hadn't gotten that right either.

"I have to go to work." She scrubbed her hands over her face as she took several more steps toward the door. Their lack of sleep was evident in the strain around her eyes. Funny, he hadn't noticed it before. Where he was getting better, she was getting worse. How could he make this right for them both? "We can talk about this tonight, okay?"

Gabriel sighed. "I'm not sure there's much more to say. Nothing will change the truth."

"You're not responsible for how you were raised, or what others did to and around you. But you sure as hell are in charge of who and what you become. When are you going to see that?" Everly shook her head.

Goliath trotted into the room, concerned by their raised voices.

Her shoulders slumped as she gave the dog a hug and ruffled his ears as if saying goodbye for more than a few hours. Gabriel barely contained his jealousy as he watched.

She looked up at him then. "Whoever you were before, you don't have to be that person anymore. It's up to you. If you don't like something about yourself, change it. I thought that's what we were doing here, but...I guess I was wrong."

No matter how much he'd thought he should protect her from himself, now that he was getting his wish, that didn't feel right either. Damn it!

"Everly—"

"I can't do this right now. Tonight," she promised before leaving his penthouse.

Though she didn't slam the door, the quiet click of it locking behind her seemed thunderous in his ears.

Goliath howled, but Everly didn't return to see what was wrong with him.

Gabriel wished he could join the dog, venting his frustration and pain. Instead he sat beside Goliath on the cold marble floor and petted him until he realized Everly was right as usual. He had to make some major adjustments. Starting with himself.

And he knew exactly what he needed to do first.

8

———

Later that afternoon Gabriel jammed one hand in his jeans pocket. With the other, he clutched the back of his neck. Was he doing the right thing? He was never quite sure anymore. Before, he'd had a set of strict rules to follow. Now he had to figure shit out on his own—or possibly with the help of Everly and some of their other friends. He drew a deep breath then prepared to knock on Casey, Jase, and Ian's door.

Before he could, it opened. Casey smiled at him. "Hey. You going to stand out there all night or do you two want to come in?"

Goliath answered for him. The dog charged past Gabriel and began to dance around Casey's feet, soaking up the attention she lavished on him. He was a celebrity in these parts.

"Casey, who's there?" Jase boomed as he left the kitchen, heading in their direction. Gabriel didn't blame the guy for being over-protective after the trouble they'd had.

"Just me." He lifted his hand in greeting.

"Hey, Gabriel." The detective grinned when he realized who it was. That alone was one hell of a gift. Hopefully what he'd come to talk about tonight didn't change the way his neighbors thought of him. That would be pretty awkward. "You're just in time. We were about to slice up this chocolate cake we got to celebrate Casey's big win in court this morning."

"Oh, congratulations." He winced. "Am I interrupting?"

Ian shouted from the kitchen, "Get in here, guys! I want some damn dessert already. I ate all my fucking vegetables at lunch, I swear."

Maybe the three of them had been about to make a snack out of Casey. Now that Gabriel had shared that experience with Everly, he knew how tasty and addicting it could be. In that case, he should leave.

"Nah, we already had a private party." Jase slapped Gabriel on the back, rattling his lungs around in his chest a bit without meaning to. "Now it's time to refuel. Seriously, join us."

He nodded.

They sat around the marble island in the chef-worthy kitchen, shoveling decadent chocolate into their faces for a few minutes before Gabriel caught Jase and Ian exchanging glances over his head. Ian spoke first. "We wish you'd drop by more often for the hell of it, but usually you keep to yourself unless Everly drags you out with her. So...uhh... Is everything okay?"

Gabriel tried not to choke on the crumbs of his cake, which suddenly seemed dry. "Fine. I guess. Well, not really. But no worse than it was before. It's just that now I think I'm ready to do something about it. And I think you guys might be able to help."

"Are you having girl trouble? This is about Everly, isn't it?" Casey scooted closer to him. "Not to be too nosey or anything, but we bumped into her leaving your apartment this morning, wearing the clothes I saw her in yesterday. It seems like maybe you two have taken some pretty big steps together. *Finally.*"

Gabriel smiled just thinking of Everly. Until he realized how close he was to ruining his chances with her. He hung his head. "Indirectly. You're right. We've been intimate and that's...incredible. But until I can get rid of some of my baggage, I don't think I have any hope of building something lasting with her."

Jase nodded. "I wondered when you were going to notice how much she wants you. She's a really sweet woman. Capable and beautiful, too. If there's chemistry between you, you should really go for it, buddy. I can tell you from experience that finding someone special only to lose them... Yeah, that sucks donkey dick."

"I've been acting like an idiot. I freely admit that." Gabriel shrugged. "I want to change that. Do something to atone for all the things I've fucked up."

"Anything can be fixed with top-quality oral. Do you need some lessons?" Ian asked. "I'm more than willing to demonstrate on Casey."

Jase smacked his partner upside the head as if he could tell how serious this was to Gabriel.

All Gabriel could think of for a moment was the night before and the schooling he'd already gotten in how to pleasure Everly. He planned to dedicate himself to practicing and perfecting his newfound skills. *If* they could work things out.

He drew an enormous breath and went for it. "That's not why I came over. I kind of wanted your professional opinions about something. I did something terrible. Might even have broken the law. I'm not sure."

The pair of detectives tensed.

"Hang on. You should probably talk to Casey alone then," Ian suggested. "If you give her a buck she won't be able to rat you out to us. I don't want you to say anything that could get you in trouble to me or Jase, okay?"

"Nah, I deserve to be punished for my wrongs." Nothing they did to him could equal the self-loathing he'd directed at himself since he'd failed to protect the victim of his fellow clergyman. The one he knew about for sure, not to mention who knew how many others...

"Gabriel, I'm sure whatever happened it wasn't intentional and it wasn't as bad as you think." Casey patted his shoulder. "Besides, we know the kind of person you really are. No one here is going to attack you or use what you tell us against you. You're safe with us. After all, we're only still here because of you and Goliath. Right, guys?"

Jase and Ian seemed less willing to commit to a blanket statement like that, but they eventually agreed. Jase said, "We definitely owe you a lot. Your quick thinking saved our lives. Why don't we speak hypothetically? Let us decide what you should do with whatever is bugging you."

That might actually make it easier to relate what had happened. Even thinking about it had the power to make Gabriel sick or angry enough to consider violence for the first time in his life.

"Someone witnessed a crime. A vile crime." He shuddered remembering the night.

Casey put her hand on his forearm and squeezed.

"A priest abusing a young boy. When they realized

what was happening, they waited just long enough to snap a few photos before interceding. While the two priests argued, the kid ran before he could be stopped or identified."

"Oh Jesus." Casey's face turned an unhealthy gray-green color that made Gabriel sure her cake wasn't sitting well anymore.

"That guy who walked in on... Anyway, he definitely didn't have anything to do with what was going on." Gabriel concentrated on unclenching his fists. He put his head in his hands as he admitted the worst of it. Angry at himself, the corrupt organization he'd supported blindly, and life in general, he dropped the pretense of anonymity. "When I tried to get the bishop to address the situation, he destroyed my evidence."

Why he hadn't been smart enough to make copies of the disgusting images before showing them to his superior? Because he'd never imagined the man would condone such evil or allow it to remain within his domain, that's why.

That fucker had known and let it slide. Hell, he could have been involved.

The more Gabriel thought about it, the more he convinced himself that was most likely. He had to speak up. To do what he could to protect the innocents he'd abandoned and any others who might wander into the trap.

"Is that why you left?" Jase asked without a hint of judgment in his tone.

"Yeah. It was coming for a while. I felt like I was waking up from a nightmare. After that they kicked me out because they realized I wasn't going to be quiet about what I'd seen. Worse, they made it seem like I'd been the one doing the abusing."

"That's a load of bullshit." Ian snorted, but Gabriel didn't find the situation humorous in the least.

"You believe me?" he asked, lifting his gaze to the two cops standing across from him. The bishop had sworn no one would and, until now, no one had. In fact, no one had even given him the chance to tell his side of the story. Even his closest contacts had mindlessly believed what they'd heard, despite it being utter bullshit.

"Of course," Jase replied without hesitation. A weight lifted off Gabriel; his chest seemed less tight for the first time in months.

"No one else has. I tried to approach several people, but no one would speak to me. The church did a fucking great job of smearing me. They made sure I'm cut off. I can't even warn anyone. I'm a pariah. I think about other times things went down around me and I wonder how many times I thought I was doing the right thing while fucking someone over." He groaned. The list of his transgressions grew day by day.

"I don't mean to offend you or your beliefs, but the church manipulated you through a long-standing system of mind-fucks." Jase shook his head. "What they do works or the organization wouldn't have lasted for literally thousands of years. I'm not trying to say everyone of faith is bad or even complicit, but at the highest levels... Yeah, most religions are designed to keep people in line. It's no wonder you were afraid to speak out."

"I wanted to go to the police, but after even people I've known my whole life refused to believe me, I thought it was pointless. I lost hope."

Jase waved him off. "It's never too late. Do you want to

write up a report of what you saw? Anything you remember could help us investigate the situation. Even if we can't identify the victim, we can start building a case against the people still left in power. If they won't protect their congregation, the odds are they're going to allow this to happen again. May even be doing it themselves. With your assistance, we could stop them from hurting anyone else."

Gabriel stared at the ceiling and blinked. Could there be someone up there listening to his prayers after all? Jase and Ian were saying everything he'd hoped for but hadn't been able to figure out how to accomplish on his own. "I'll do anything I can. Even go back there if you need me to."

"Let's start with a report." Ian grabbed a notebook off the counter and handed it to Gabriel, who spent the better part of an hour flooding the pages with as many details as he could recall. The act of writing it down, getting it out of his mind, seemed to ease some of his misery as if he'd drained a toxic, festering wound.

It seemed simple now. They were right. He'd been brainwashed, his thoughts knotted up with fear and doubt about even the most fundamental concepts of right and wrong. It had taken months for him to begin sorting everything out on his own.

Eventually he dropped the pen and slid his report across the counter to Jase. He slumped, exhausted.

Casey put her hand over his fingers and squeezed. "Can I ask you something personal? You don't have to answer if you don't want to." She waited for him to decide, making him even more comfortable sharing with her.

"Sure."

"Is this one of the things that's been holding you back from giving all of yourself to Everly?" She blushed, then grinned. "I couldn't help but notice the marks on her neck this morning or the missing button on her shirt. Still, she seemed...a lot more tense than someone who'd spent the night tearing the sheets up with a new lover."

"We argued before she left." He sighed. "Half the time I think I'm damned for turning my back on my old life. The other half, I think I'm tainted for having been a part of it. Each day I spend with Everly makes me want things I don't deserve. And now, I'm not sure what she's expecting. I feel different. Stronger. And that makes me want even more. Maybe that's not what she signed up for. Maybe she liked the broken me. Except she's fixing me. I'm freaked out that I'm going to become someone she's not into."

"A bit of advice... Don't let her hear you talking like that." Jase crossed his arms. "She's fierce in her own way. Adventurous and unrelenting. She's strong enough to stand by your side once she doesn't have to help you get back up anymore. Someday you're going to be there to return the favor."

Damn straight. Had Gabriel insulted her by worrying too much? Fuck. He bet he had. The only way to make it up to her was to stop trying to protect her and let her see the parts of him he was hiding, even from himself.

"Now that I've had a taste of her, I need more. A lot more. Things I'm not sure she'd be into. Worse would be if I scared her off or hurt her. That would kill me. You really think she's up for it?"

"Only she can say." Jase raised his hands then let them drop. "I mean, Everly is a super-sweet girl, but that doesn't mean she doesn't have a naughty side. Don't assume you know what people do in their bedrooms. As long as it's consensual and you're both having fun, go for it."

"So you think she'd respond well if I took charge in

the bedroom?" He couldn't believe he was asking them this. "She seemed to like being my first. Teaching me how to pleasure her and stuff—"

"Hang on, *Everly* popped your cherry?" Ian braced himself, splaying his hands on the countertop. "Wow."

"Of course, that makes sense." Casey smiled warmly at him. "You were a priest. It's just so difficult for me to think of you like that sometimes. You know, you've changed a lot already even if you don't realize it."

"Well, now you know why we're making up for lost time." Gabriel couldn't help the smirk that tipped his lips up. The nights he'd spent getting lost in her had been the best hours of his life. He couldn't wait to do more, go further, if that was something she'd be into.

"Oh, now there's a look I know very well. Look out, Everly." Casey chuckled.

"I guess that's what I'm worried about..." Gabriel's amusement vanished. "Do you think she's into submissive guys? Or will she like it if I take a more aggressive role now that she's made me more comfortable and confident and...*hungry*?"

"I'm betting she'd be up for that. I mean, you should probably ask her or give it a try and see how she responds." Ian winked. "I'd be happy to lend you my handcuffs."

Gabriel groaned at that. The vision of Everly bound to his bed, spread out for him to ravish as he saw fit, made it impossible for him to get up and move from behind the island any time soon. Unless he wanted the trio of his neighbors to see exactly what even the mere thought of having Everly at his mercy did to him.

"Embrace your instincts. Be the man you want to be. The man you always should have been. Think for yourself. Take pride in your strength. Nothing is stopping you out here. Nothing but your own mind. It's okay, Gabriel." Casey closed the gap between them and hugged him tight. "All kidding aside, I think you should know that we adore you. Everly does, too. We admire you for having the courage to revolutionize yourself when you realized you weren't on the right path for you, and for what you're doing to try to stop innocent children from being hurt."

"I know you're going to hate this..." Jase winced. "But you were one of those children, too, Gabriel. They may never have laid a hand on you, but still, these people raised you. They groomed you when your mind was impressionable. You never really had a choice. So cut yourself a break."

Gabriel reflexively rejected that revelation for a moment, until it sank in that Jase was one-hundred percent right. The things he'd been taught formed a foundation that even now he couldn't fully see. He'd had to tear himself down, smash himself into rubble before he could begin to rebuild.

Ian added his two cents to the silence, which was growing long enough to be somewhat awkward. What did they expect when they'd help him strip back even more layers? "Don't let the old you keep the new you from being completely happy. You've already sacrificed too much to half-ass this now. Go get what you really want. Show Everly who you are, and either that works for her or it doesn't. But you'll both know, so you can either take things to the next level or find someone who accepts you as you are. Because despite what you've said, you're wrong. You deserve to be loved. Everyone does."

"How'd you get so damn smart?" Casey crossed to Ian and swooped in for a kiss that would have made Gabriel uncomfortable a week ago. Today it only made him miss Everly. "It took me a while to figure that shit out." She shook her head as if in apology to one of the loves of her life.

Jase turned to Gabriel then. "I don't want you to make the same mistakes I did. Don't let Everly go because you think there's something wrong with the way you're made. By some miracle, it could be that what you want and what she needs are exactly the same thing."

"All I really want is her." Gabriel gripped the countertop hard enough to turn his knuckles white. "I'll do anything, be anything, she wants to have her."

"What I'm saying is if it's right, all you need to do is be true to yourself," Casey reminded him. It would take a while to keep from falling into old habits. "And I have a super good feeling that you two were meant to find each other."

"I'm not sure I believe in destiny or divine guidance anymore, but maybe I finally just got lucky." Gabriel smiled. "Thank you. All of you. I'd better get going if I'm going to be ready to do this when she gets off work."

"Either way we've got plenty of cake. So come by after and let us know if it's for a celebration or to drown your sorrows." Casey held up her hands and crossed her fingers.

Gabriel nodded. "I'll do that. I hope you're right. Thanks, seriously."

"We've always got your back," she told him. "I'm betting you'll have Everly with you when you stop by for a midnight snack."

"I hope you're right." He shook the hand Jase held out to him before tugging his neighbor into a one-armed man hug.

"It gives us a lot of comfort knowing you're here on the nights we're out working. I know you'd do anything to protect Casey and she knows she can trust you," Ian said quietly. "If you were really the man you're afraid you are, that wouldn't be the case."

Their high opinion did a lot to boost Gabriel's confidence. That was good. Because he was going to need a ton to take the next step on his journey to reclaim his life and live it on his own terms. Hopefully, with Everly by his side.

9

E verly knocked quietly, then let herself in to Gabriel's apartment. Whether he wanted to talk or not, she had a few things she had to get off her chest. Only then would she leave it to him to decide if he truly planned to push her away so he could wallow in his self-pity again.

If he did, it would be for good this time.

She had some pride, damn it. Intentionally or not, he shredded it each time he refused to see that she was capable of helping him tame his demons. What if he could never break free of the traps the church had set in his mind to control him?

Her breath caught in her chest when she noticed him standing with his hands at head height, palms flat on the wall of glass. He stared out at the world, as if he didn't quite fit in with the rest of the mere mortals below him.

The sunset flared, setting the sky on fire. It limned him in a blaze of light. Though she'd never been a religious person, she might have believed he could be some sort of avenging angel right then.

"Gabriel." She approached him cautiously from behind, practically tiptoeing into his personal space. Tension crackled around them. Something had changed. The man in front of her was not the damaged one she'd come to know over the past few months or the tentative one she'd introduced to physical intimacy this past week.

He was formidable, righteous, reborn with a core of steel that hadn't bent despite being subjected to enormous pressures. She should probably be wary. Instead, she was drawn to him, unable to stay away.

From the couch, Goliath looked up at her without lifting his massive head. His forlorn expression hit her. Even the dog knew a storm was brewing.

Could she divert Gabriel from the destructive spiral he'd been sliding down and embrace whatever this emerging side of him was? She wanted to do that more than she'd wanted to graduate at the top of her class or be the youngest manager in the 150-year history of Beekman Place.

Saving him had become her mission. Now it finally looked as if he might be ready to save himself. Where would that leave them?

Gabriel didn't respond when she called out to him.

He didn't budge.

So she crept closer, until she could wrap her arms around his waist and rest her cheek between his shoulder blades. The sculpted back she had admired so often recently impressed her and reminded her that he wasn't as vulnerable as he sometimes seemed.

"Hey, I'm here." Would that make him feel any better?

"For the first time...I think I am, too," he rasped.

"I get that you have a lot to work through still. Maybe even more after the things we've done this week. It's going to take time and there will be setbacks. I just want you to know that I'm here for you. And I'd like to make your life better, not more painful. So if you need me to go, to back off, so you can sort things out on your own..." She began to peel her fingers from his abdomen, one by one.

Until his hand flashed downward and covered hers completely.

"I don't want you to leave." He whipped around, and dropped his head until he spoke nearly against her lips. She shivered. "But I understand if you do. Being with you, experimenting, it's unlocked a lot of desires I didn't even know I had. I don't think they're going to disappear any time soon now that they're unleashed. I'm not sure that's really what you planned to sign up for. Dealing with the darker parts of me not only for a wild night or two but all the time. Forever."

"Fuck that. You don't get to decide what I'm into. Can't you see I love all of you, Gabriel?" Uh oh. How had that slipped past the lock she'd put on her heart and right out of her mouth? Jeez. Now he was going to wall himself off for sure. "I respect you. I'm attracted to you, too. But it aggravates me when you either don't see what I see when I look at you or you think I'm not strong enough to handle it."

"Stop right there." He gripped her tighter, his hand snaking around to the back of her neck and sending tingles down her spine. "I never thought you were weak. I don't think that."

"Then you understand that I want to be the person to help you discover who you really are. Deep down. Beneath the scars and the robes you've had to hide them beneath all your life. Show me, Gabriel. I can handle it. I can handle you. In fact, I *need* you."

"I pray you're right. Because I can't resist temptation any longer. If you stay, we'll find out together what I'm capable of when I quit holding back."

Instead of responding, Everly wrenched from his hold long enough to begin undoing the buttons of her blouse. Gabriel made a harsh sound in his throat, raw enough to draw a whimper from Goliath.

When she turned her head to reassure the dog that everything was fine, Gabriel pounced. He grabbed her wrist and swapped their positions, pressing her face-first against the glass. He tucked his fingers in the partially opened neckline of her shirt and yanked, scattering buttons so that they pinged off the window in every direction before he smooshed her back into place.

The shock of the cool, smooth, hard surface against her breasts, even through her thin lace bra, and the rest of her torso made her gasp. She attempted to shift away from the shocking contact, but Gabriel stopped her with a single firm touch on her shoulder along with a growled warning.

"Stay where I put you."

She did as he instructed while he removed her skirt and underwear but left her heels. He did seem to have a thing for them. Everly made a mental note to buy even taller ones next time. Subconsciously, she shifted from foot to foot.

Gabriel didn't miss her small movement. His open palm landed on her bare ass with a spank that reverberated through the penthouse, standing her nerves at attention. Who the hell was this guy and what had he done with her sweet, sad Gabriel?

She had no idea, but she decided she liked him.

A lot.

The distinct sound of a zipper being undone with a single yank caught her attention. She didn't make the mistake of trying to peek over her shoulder at Gabriel as he freed his cock from his jeans. Instead, she stood and waited for him to give it to her, when he was ready.

Lord knew she was. The glow of his palm on her ass had guaranteed that.

"What are you thinking, Everly?"

"That I wish you'd save the talking for later."

He spanked her again, this time on the other cheek. "That's not very nice."

"I need you," she blurted. "You're not going to leave me like this, are you? Hurry."

He chuckled. The rich, deep sound thrilled her. "Last night I realized something about myself. I'm a little bit of an asshole. I can attest that waiting won't kill you. It'll only make you hungrier when you get what you want."

She started to object, but he silenced her with another slap on her ass.

This one was followed by his foot nudging hers wider apart and then the blunt head of his cock, which spread her as it invaded her pussy in a single, deep thrust. She'd never been so glad she was on birth control as she was at that moment. Stopping him even long enough to put a condom on would have killed her. Waiting to discuss the situation with him, when he obviously hadn't even realized the potential repercussions of his actions due to his history...just...no.

Fuck now, talk later.

Gabriel pinned her to the window with his body. It plastered against her from head to toe.

She loved being sandwiched between him and the glass. Let everyone watch, she didn't give a shit. Then they would know, like she did, what perfect counterparts they were.

"I'm not joking, Everly. I'm possessive. I want you to myself. Is that going to be a problem? If I make you mine and only mine? No more sharing."

She moaned. "Not as long as you keep fucking me like that."

"Of course I will." He leaned and nipped her ear before whispering into it. "Because you have all of me, too. Unconditionally. Fair's fair, after all."

EVERLY'S THIGHS QUIVERED. If he hadn't been holding her in place, she might have slid to the floor. No chance he was letting her go anywhere now unless it was lower on his cock.

"Yes. Gabriel, yes." She sank the slightest bit, sheathing him completely. "I love it when you embrace your inner sinner."

Could she have been attracted to the parts of him he'd tried so desperately to hide from her all this time? How was that possible?

He wasn't about to stop and wonder right then.

Couldn't. Because everything in him compelled him to fuck. To mate with her in every sense of the word. He wanted to be her partner. In bed and in life.

Gabriel curled his toes in the carpet and began to thrust. He wedged his hands between her breasts and the glass so he could squeeze her breasts, letting them overflow his palms.

He didn't try to stifle the animalistic sounds he made

as he drove up into her again and again. Especially not when she responded in kind.

It didn't take long before her pussy was sucking at his dick, trying to lure him into ending their session early. Before he could withdraw and find a way to amuse himself while he backed away from the edge, she shrieked.

Gabriel didn't know what possessed him then, but he leaned down and sucked on the sensitive spot he'd discovered on her neck the night before. The instant he did, she lost it.

Everly thrashed against the glass, trying to climb it or fly or who knew what. All she did was manage to impale herself repeatedly on his cock, enhancing her sudden orgasm.

Gabriel was glad he'd jacked off several times before she was due to get off work. Otherwise he probably would have fallen over the edge into rapture with her.

This way was far more fun.

He lifted her into his arms but didn't make it farther than the kitchen before he felt the undeniable compulsion to be joined with her again. So he bent her over the kitchen counter and pinned her wrists in the small of her back. They made an excellent grip. He anchored her with them as he rode her to a second, if weaker, release.

"Gabriel? What is this? What's gotten into you?" She sounded dazed, but not afraid. Surprised, but not disgusted.

"*You* have. Let's go." He spun her around and lifted her again, cupping her ass. She wrapped her arms and legs around him, hugging him as he carried her a little farther into his lair. He had to stop again, several times, to feel her pussy clasping him, urging him deeper, reassuring him that she found him attractive no matter how nasty he got with her.

Against the hallway wall. Up the stairs. And even once on the floor of the sitting room in his master suite. He couldn't seem to make it as far as the bed before plunging back inside her and using his cock, his hands, and his dirty words to undo her further.

When he finally did get her to his bed, he was at his limit. Breaks or no breaks, he was going to come inside her this time. Instead of letting her ride him, or making love to her face-to-face—slowly, gently—he arranged her on her hands and knees.

Face down, ass up, she tempted him beyond restraint.

Gabriel mounted her and sank balls-deep.

She shouted his name as she rocked back against him. He wrapped his fist in her hair and angled her head so he could carefully read her expression as he took them somewhere he'd never been. It was a place he'd love to visit often. A place where he was powerful. A place where his desire brought Everly unfathomable pleasure. A place where nothing mattered except the slap of their bodies meeting over and over. Coming together.

He put one hand on her lower back to keep her in place while the other snaked around beneath her to rub her pussy and feel the place where he disappeared into her. He was getting close, and this time, today especially, he needed her to shatter with him.

His middle finger hadn't made very many circles around her clit before she began to chant his name. Her body gathered around him.

When she trembled, about to come on his pounding cock, he pressed the thumb of his hand on her back against her asshole. All that porn-watching he'd done earlier after following Colton's emailed recommendations seemed to pay off when she came. The epic orgasm rattled her from toes to teeth.

She quaked around him, squeezing violently until he had no chance at resistance.

Gabriel threw back his head and roared. He gave Everly every bit of his cock, his come, and his heart. He hoped she understood the fierce release she'd driven him to wasn't only about sex. She'd freed him from the shackles he'd put on himself and he planned to repay her for it every day of his life.

With the frantic energy leeching out of him, he sagged, blanketing Everly's back. He nuzzled her nape and memorized the smell of her along with the way he felt in that single blindingly euphoric moment.

Until he realized that she was trembling beneath him.

Gabriel freed himself from her body, making them both groan. Then he gathered her into his arms and sat, cradling her in his lap. "Are you okay, Everly?"

She nodded, though her lower lip wobbled. "If you dare to apologize right now I'm going to go nuts on you. Don't ruin it, Gabriel. Please. It was the best sex of my life."

"Mine, too," he said with a wry grin.

Everly lost it. She cracked up until her eyes shined with love and laughter and bone-deep contentment. Eventually she settled, staring up at him with wonder before snuggling up against his chest with a sigh.

"What was that look for?" he wondered. At least it wasn't one of abject horror.

"It's just like I'm meeting you for the first time." She ran her hands over his chest then down his arms in a repetitive pattern that lulled him. "The you I always sensed was there."

"Me, too. I still need to do a lot of soul searching. About my faith and what I believe in. About the universe and what sort of higher power might exist, if any. Most especially about how I can keep doing the sort of work I thought I was doing before, helping people overcome whatever their challenges are in this life. Now that I have practically unlimited resources, I should be able to do something meaningful with them. Maybe put together a refuge program for people fleeing cults or those recovering from abuse. Anything that might make up in some small way for damage I might have been complicit in causing."

"Those all sound like amazing ideas." Everly's nose twitched as if she was trying not to burst into sobs. "This is the first time I've heard you talking about moving forward. I'm proud of you, Gabriel. It won't be easy, but you're going to get there. You'll figure this out."

"I'll tell you one thing I still believe in without reservation." He brushed aside a wisp of her hair to press a gentle kiss to her forehead.

Everly's throat flexed as if she couldn't manage to speak. Hopefully, she could already tell what he was going to say by the piercing clarity of his eyes, fully unveiled to her for the first time. He wished she could see straight into his soul and read the truth there. Maybe she could.

"I believe in us. I have faith in you. You saved me. I love you, too, Everly." He framed her face with his hands and held her as if she were more precious than the diamond-encrusted Bible in the showcase downstairs when he sipped from her bruised lips. Because she was. "You're like a light. From the first time I met you, you were able to brighten the darkest times of my life. When I thought I'd never see the sun again, you proved me wrong. I hope you don't mind being the day to my night, because I don't think this damage is going to go away anytime soon. It still hurts."

She hugged him then, tight enough that he had trouble finishing his thoughts.

"But it hurts way less when you're with me."

"That's the nicest thing anyone has ever said to me." She attempted to blink away her tears, but they spilled over anyway. So he kissed them away.

"Does that mean you'll move in with us—me and Goliath, I mean?" Sure, it might have been too soon to ask. But Gabriel was approaching the situation with unflinching optimism. She seemed to think it looked good on him.

"Um...hell yes! Besides the fact that I am obsessed with this building and have been saving up for my own place here, I don't ever want to be apart from you again. You make my life better, too. You know that right?"

Gabriel paused. He truly hadn't considered what *he* did for *her* other than their recent bedroom games. "How?"

"You look out for me, take care of me, listen to me, have fun with me, love me... You're everything I've ever dreamed of and more."

"In that case..." Gabriel grinned. "Goliath! Here, boy!"

The dog was at their side in an instant, bounding onto the bed with hardly a limp. Like his master, he was overcoming his war wounds. He barked and covered their faces with excited doggie kisses while they laughed together.

"Welcome home, Everly."

MORE PENTHOUSE PLEASURES

Check out the rest of the Penthouse Pleasures books for five more stories about Gabriel's neighbors.

Taboo

Kinky

Sinner

Mentor

Voyeur

Fetish

EXCERPT FROM TABOO

PENTHOUSE PLEASURES #1

"Congratulations, you're officially the newest resident of Beekman Place. Welcome home, Ms. Clark." The cheery front desk manager plopped a set of golden keys in Casey's palm. Okay, so they probably weren't *really* gold, but gold-toned and shiny as fuck. They gleamed like everything else in the fancy lobby.

Major goal achieved. Hashtag success.

Casey officially lived in one of the most prestigious neighborhoods in Manhattan. Take that, humble beginnings.

After thanking the manager, she twirled her new keys around her index finger, careful not to mess up her perfect manicure as she headed for the private elevator that led to the penthouse apartments on the highest floor of the iconic building. The ride straight to the top in the polished car seemed surreal.

The woman reflected in the mirrors—with her stylish blonde hair, perfect makeup, and designer suit—was a far cry from the bedraggled white trash girl Casey had been before she'd known better. Only her wide, bright blue eyes seemed the same to her.

Could this really be her life?

Damn straight it was. Just because she'd grown up in a trailer park on the outskirts of some Podunk upstate town didn't mean she didn't belong here. After all, she'd spent the past twenty years busting her ass to make up for that inauspicious start.

She'd sacrificed everything for this.

Casey swallowed hard as she thought of her mom. Lorna had drank herself to death before Casey could afford the fees for a fancy rehab facility. Not that her mother would have agreed to go anyway. Then there was the one guy she'd pictured herself spending the rest of her life with.

She scrunched her eyes closed until the unwanted ghosts of loved ones lost dissolved.

A cheery *bing* announced her arrival at the top. Casey exited the elevator and crossed the wide hallway to her penthouse's door.

She aligned her freshly cut key with the lock. This was it. The moment she fulfilled the promise to her younger self about where she'd live when she grew up—a home without wheels, someplace classy. An apartment where she didn't have to lie awake at night wondering if one of the neighbors would bust through her window and hurt her. Or worse, if her own mother would sell her to them for a six-pack.

Her fingers shook as she slid it home and shoved open the door.

Head high, shoulders back, she marched inside the penthouse apartment.

Her penthouse apartment.

Sure, she'd only been able to afford it because the previous owner had vanished along with his long-overdue mortgage payments. The bank had been eager to cut her a deal on the place. Nobody had to know that, though.

Could that be why her victory seemed so hollow? Because it wasn't quite what it appeared?

Fuck that. It was still a huge accomplishment.

She hated the part of her that would never be satisfied, the side that constantly struggled to prove she was better than her roots. The piece that was a slave to ambition.

It wasn't that there was anything wrong with growing up in a trailer park. Not in and of itself. It was the specific bottom-of-the-barrel neighborhood and the defeatist mentality that her mother had reveled in that had been the problem. Casey couldn't stand the thought of succumbing to those innate tendencies. There had been plenty of times when she'd felt like giving up, slinking home, and learning to settle for something simple. Easy. A comfortable existence with the boy she'd fled from.

No. She refused to give in to the weakness she'd inherited.

Feet spread wide in five-inch spike heels, hands on hips, and shoulders back, Casey tossed her mane over her shoulder. She admired the city laid out before her like it was her domain. Hers for the taking. Except she'd already conquered it.

She'd graduated Columbia Law School in the top one percent of her class before a major venture capital firm recruited her to join their team as a corporate lawyer specializing in mergers and acquisitions. So far she'd been instrumental in seven takeovers and had even earned shares of the businesses she'd helped take over. Just last month, she'd been promoted to the head of her department when her mentor had retired.

It would have been easier to climb the outside of the sleek skyscraper she now called home. At times she felt like she'd clung to the path upward by her fingernails. But it had been worth it.

It was one of those moments—the defining sort—in a woman's life. Or it should have been.

Instead, Casey stood at the floor-to-ceiling windows, staring out onto the city far below her while wondering how she fit in. From way up here, everything seemed so distant, separate from the heights she'd struggled to elevate herself to.

Had she taken things too far?

Maybe there was more to life than work, promotions to more stressful positions, and ever-increasing bonuses. A fancy car, expensive meals at world-class restaurants, and even a luxurious penthouse apartment didn't mean as much if there wasn't anyone around to share her success with.

She wished her mom was here to see it, even if she would've been too drunk to understand the momentousness of the occasion.

A companion of the sexy male variety to share it with would be nice, too.

Casey promised herself she'd build an online dating profile and at least take a peek at a few eligible bachelors as soon as she'd finished unpacking and settling in. It could be fun to focus on finding a partner who could enjoy the perks of her newfound lifestyle. Someone to cheer her on and be proud of her accomplishments. Someone she could do the same for.

Otherwise, what was the point of having all this?

Getting laid couldn't hurt either. It'd been far too long since she'd had a decent orgasm provided by an actual man instead of a battery-operated boyfriend.

There she went thinking about the guy she'd left behind. Sure, he'd been gruff and immature, wild and crass. He'd also been gorgeous, and fucked like no one she'd been with since.

Casey rubbed her palm over her stomach, trying to squash out the emptiness there.

She nearly convinced herself it was simply hunger. After she'd finished devouring delivery from the top sushi joint in the city and the emptiness lingered, she knew it was something a lot harder to fix.

Well, shitcakes.

Click HERE to keep reading Taboo.

EXCERPT FROM KINKY

Kent stepped into the police station and walked to the desk.

"I'm Kent Grayson. I was called about a young woman named Christina Mills."

"Oh, yeah," the sergeant said. "Detective Rosco wants to talk to you. He'll be right out."

Kent paced. He wasn't used to being kept waiting, and ordinarily he'd have one of his staff handle this sort of thing. Not that this exact sort of thing had ever happened before. He didn't usually consort with the type of person who got picked up by the police in the middle of the night.

But Christina was the daughter of an old friend and she was in trouble.

"Mr. Grayson."

Kent looked up to see a man in torn jeans and a leather jacket, full beard walking toward him.

"I'm Detective Rosco," he said as he held out his hand and Kent shook it. "I understand you're Ms. Mills stepfather."

Kent didn't allow the shock of that statement to affect his expression.

"Where is Christina? Is she all right?"

He couldn't help remembering the last time he saw Christina. Her long blonde hair swept back from her face, held by a clip at the back of her head. Her heart-shaped lips turned up in a smile that set her innocent face aglow. It had been her sixteenth birthday and he'd come to visit so he could give her a special gift.

She'd always been fascinated by the fact he lived in New York City. She'd loved the idea of living somewhere as exciting as New York. It was all she'd ever talked about. So he'd given her a necklace with the I Love NY logo in gold. When she'd opened it, her eyes had gone wide and she'd thrown her arms around him.

"She's fine." The detective led Kent through a door, then down a hallway. "But she's gotten herself into some trouble. That's why I wanted to have a talk with you."

As they walked, Kent saw several women sitting on a bench in a waiting room. Hookers by the look of them in their skimpy, suggestive clothing. One young woman's gaze locked on him and she stood up.

Fuck, she was stunning, despite the slutty dress she wore. Her hair cascaded over her shoulders in sunny waves and the tight dress that hugged her perfect body was cut low in front, showing the generous swell of her creamy breasts. And it was so short it showed every inch of her long, shapely legs.

She surged toward him.

"Daddy," she cried as she threw her arms around him.

What the fuck?

Then he realized. *This* was Christina.

"Please," she whispered desperately against his ear. "I told them you're my stepfather. Please go along with it."

Fuck, he could barely think straight. She was clearly distraught and he'd wrapped his arms around her in an automatic need to comfort her, but his body tightened at the feel of her breasts pushed tight against him. Making him want things he shouldn't want. Tickling a need buried so deep inside him, he dared not let it loose.

He grasped her shoulders and eased her back, then gazed into her shimmering green eyes.

"Christina, what's going on?"

"I'm sorry, Daddy. It's not as bad as what they're going to tell you."

He narrowed his eyes. One, he wished she'd stopped calling him Daddy because... damn it... it was seriously messing with his head. Two, how the hell had the sweet young girl he'd known become... a prostitute?

"Sit down, Ms. Mills," Detective Rosco said to her. "Mr. Grayson, let's talk."

He led Kent to a room with a table and closed the door.

"She told us you're her stepfather but that you and her mother are separated. She didn't know how to get in touch with you."

"I haven't seen her or her mother for several years. So what is she being charged with?"

"We picked her up outside a bar for soliciting. We have one witness. The guy we caught talking to her. He said she came on to him, offering to go back to his hotel room for money."

Detective Rosco leaned back in his chair.

"She has no priors, but she also has no permanent address and no job." He leaned forward. "I know this must be disturbing for you. I just want to say that I've seen a lot of young woman on the street but whatever's going on with her isn't that bad. Yet."

The thought of Christina fucking men for money seemed pretty bad to Kent. In fact, the thought ate away at his gut, making him feel sick.

The detective leaned forward, looking Kent square in the eyes.

"I think there's still time to straighten her out and get her back on the right track. *If* you're willing to get involved. I could put her in jail, but I'd rather turn her over to you. If you'll agree to give her the time and effort to try and turn her around."

"And what do you have in mind?"

"I'd like you to agree to keep her with you for no less than a month. Spend time with her. Show her you care. Maybe she just needs some stability."

"I can do that."

"Good. I'm glad to hear that."

Click HERE to keep reading Kinky.

Nothing's sexier than men with power tools.

Sultry summer heat has nothing on the five-man crew renovating the house next door. No one could blame Kate for leaning out the window for a better view of the manscape. The nasty fall that follows isn't part of her fantasy—but the man who saves her from splattering the sidewalk is definitely the star.

When Mike personally attends to her injuries, she realizes her white knight in a hard hat has a tender side, giving her no choice but to surrender to the lust that's been arcing between them since day one. In the aftermath of the best sex of her life, she whispers her most secret desire: to be ravaged by his crew.

She never expected Mike would dare her to take what she wants—or that the freedom to make her most decadent desires come true could be the foundation for something lasting...

Warning: This book may cause you to spontaneously combust as five hot guys bring a woman's wildest fantasies to life during one blazing summer affair.

Excerpt From Kate's Crew:

Kate wiped her palms on her paint-splattered cutoffs before adjusting her grip on the rebuilt window casement. A flash of tan skin drew her attention to glistening muscles. They rippled over five sexy frames as the crew renovating the townhouse next door hammered nail after nail into their first-story roof, just a few feet below her perch.

From inside the bedroom where she worked, she inched to the edge of the ladder rung then craned her neck through the opening in front of her for a glimpse of the intricate tattoo spanning Mike's broad shoulders. Instead, she caught him reaching up to their stash of supplies for another pack of shingles. When her gaze latched onto the drop of sweat that slid along his neck, she forgot to breathe. She watched in fascination as it journeyed over his defined pecs and six-pack abs. After it was absorbed in the ultra-low-riding jeans snugged to his trim hips by a bulging tool belt, she heaved a sigh of relief.

Kate swiped at a blob of paint that had plopped onto her wrist unnoticed while she'd ogled Mike. Her tongue moistened her lips as she imagined licking a similar trail down his body. The edge of the fresh trim gouged her thigh as she strained for a better view. The gasp she made busted her. His head lifted, catching her spying. Great, now she'd never convince him to take it easy with his persistent innuendo or date invites. And, no matter how much she wanted to, she couldn't indulge either of their desires.

Mike threw her a dazzling victory grin. The anticipation sparkling in his cocky stare blasted a shockwave through her, screwing with her balance. The ladder wobbled then tipped. She probably could have righted herself if she hadn't been standing on tiptoes to maximize her view of the scenery. In slow motion, she watched his expression morph from flirtatious to horrified.

Kate flung out her arms in an attempt to catch the frame before she tumbled through it but the momentum swung her around. Her temple grazed the custom-made pewter latch she'd installed the day before. She hung, suspended in midair, as Mike rose from his crouch. The other guys began to turn toward her, but he was already sprinting for the edge.

Terror froze her insides when he launched himself across the ten-foot gap between their houses. Then she spun away, losing sight of him. She braced for imminent impact.

Shit, this is going to hurt.

Everything happened at once. Air whooshed from her lungs when she slammed, on her side, onto the roof. She rolled, flexing her ankles in an attempt to find purchase that would halt her skid toward the brink. But her knee wrenched at an awkward angle while she continued to rake over the slate. Her hand caught the ridge of an attic vent, slowing her descent, but gravity overcame the tenuous hold. Her frantic fingers recoiled from the sharp metal edge.

The gutters rushed closer, her last hope. After that, she'd have to pray the evergreen shrubs would cushion her, preventing any broken bones. The heels of her work boots hit the aluminum edging but kept going. Her legs dangled in thin air.

Then a strong hand banded around her wrist. Her arm nearly jerked from the socket as she lurched to a stop. Kate shoved on the edging shingles with her free hand, fighting to stay on the roof.

"Son of a bitch!" Mike hauled her the rest of the way up.

To keep reading Kate's Crew, click here.

NAUGHTY NEWS

Want to win cool stuff? Get sneak peeks of upcoming books? How about being the first to know what's in the pipeline or where Jayne will be making appearances near you? If any of that stuff sounds good then sign up for Jayne's newsletter, the Naughty News. She never shares you information, pinky swear!

www.jaynerylon.com/newsletter

WHAT WAS YOUR FAVORITE PART?

Did you enjoy this book? If so, please leave a review and tell your friends about it. Word of mouth and online reviews are immensely helpful and greatly appreciated.

JAYNE'S SHOP

Check out Jayne's online shop for autographed print books, direct download ebooks, reading-themed apparel up to size 5XL, mugs, tote bags, notebooks, Mr. Rylon's wood (you'll have to see it for yourself!) and more.
www.jaynerylon.com/shop

LISTEN UP!

The majority of Jayne's books are also available in audio format on Audible, Amazon and iTunes.

ABOUT THE AUTHORS

Jayne Rylon is a New York Times and USA Today bestselling author. She received the 2011 Romantic Times Reviewers' Choice Award for Best Indie Erotic Romance. Her stories used to begin as daydreams in seemingly endless business meetings, but now she is a full time author, who employs the skills she learned from her straight-laced corporate existence in the business of writing. She lives in Ohio with two cats and her husband, the infamous Mr. Rylon. When she can escape her purple office, she loves to travel the world, avoid speeding tickets in her beloved Sky, and–of course–read.

Opal Carew is the author of over a dozen romance stories in which she makes offerings of hope, success, and love to her readers. Opal loves crystals, dragons, feathers, cats, pink hair, the occult, Manga artwork, and all that glitters. She earned a degree in Mathematics from the University of Waterloo, and spent 15 years as a software analyst before turning to her passions as a writer. Opal lives with her husband and two teen-aged sons in Ontario, Canada

New York Times and USA Today bestselling author Avery Aster pens The Manhattanites, a contemporary erotic romance series of full-length, stand-alone novels, and the naughty new adult prequel companion series The Undergrad Years. As a resident of New York City and a graduate from New York University, Avery gives readers an inside look at the city's glitzy nightlife, socialite sexcapades and tall tales of the über-rich and ultra-famous.

ALSO BY JAYNE RYLON

MEN IN BLUE

Hot Cops Save Women In Danger

Night is Darkest

Razor's Edge

Mistress's Master

Spread Your Wings

Wounded Hearts

Bound For You

DIVEMASTERS

Sexy SCUBA Instructors By Day, Doms On A Mega-Yacht By Night

Going Down

Going Deep

Going Hard

POWERTOOLS

Five Guys Who Get It On With Each Other & One Girl. Enough Said?

Kate's Crew

Morgan's Surprise

Kayla's Gift

Devon's Pair

Nailed to the Wall

Hammer it Home

HOT RODS

Powertools Spin Off. Keep up with the Crew plus...

Seven Guys & One Girl. Enough Said?

King Cobra

Mustang Sally

Super Nova

Rebel on the Run

Swinger Style

Barracuda's Heart

Touch of Amber

Long Time Coming

STANDALONE

Menage

Middleman

4-Ever Theirs

Nice & Naughty

Contemporary

Where There's Smoke

Report For Booty

COMPASS BROTHERS

Modern Western Family Drama Plus Lots Of Steamy Sex

Northern Exposure

Southern Comfort

Eastern Ambitions

Western Ties

COMPASS GIRLS

Daughters Of The Compass Brothers Drive Their Dads Crazy And Fall In Love

Winter's Thaw

Hope Springs

Summer Fling

Falling Softly

PLAY DOCTOR

Naughty Sexual Psychology Experiments Anyone?

Dream Machine

Healing Touch

RED LIGHT

A Hooker Who Loves Her Job

Complete Red Light Series Boxset

FREE - Through My Window - FREE

Star

Can't Buy Love

Free For All

PICK YOUR PLEASURES

Choose Your Own Adventure Romances!

Pick Your Pleasure

Pick Your Pleasure 2

RACING FOR LOVE

MMF Menages With Race-Car Driver Heroes

Complete Series Boxset

Driven

Shifting Gears

PARANORMALS

Vampires, Witches, And A Man Trapped In A Painting

Paranormal Double Pack Boxset

Picture Perfect

Reborn

www.ingramcontent.com/pod-product-compliance
Lightning Source LLC
Chambersburg PA
CBHW060747210726
48292CB00015B/2813